'Are you all right?' The question sounded more desperate than she had intended it to. The words 'I'm sorry' hovered on her tongue, but she didn't have a chance to get them out.

'You'll have to hit me a damn sight harder than that if you want to finish me off, Sister Newington.' James said. 'You're crazy, did you know that? You can get away with all sorts of things by classing them under the title of women's oppression. You can call me all the names you like, hit me, ruin my reputation in public, and all in the name of Women's Liberation!'

'How dare you?' cried Nina. 'Just like a man, turning it all back on us. I suppose it's *my* fault that you came to see this dirty little peep-show today?'

'It's women like you that make men into sexists,' James retorted. 'I'm getting out of here, and you're not going to stop me.'

'Grrr!' All thoughts of apology fled from her now. 'I am!' Without thought for what she was doing, Nina batted him round the head again with the placard. He grabbed it from her and broke it efficiently into two over his knee—and at that moment the policeman arrived . . .

Holly North was born in Cambridge in 1955. She read History at Durham University and in 1978 married her American husband, Sam. His career has taken them all over the world, from New York and Paris to Saudi Arabia and, at the moment, Japan. Holly teaches English and restores oriental carpets when she can—and when she can't, she keeps herself sane by writing about her home country. She's a passionate advocate of the NHS, which looks all the more impressive from abroad, and consults her brother-in-law, who is a paediatrician, for much of the medical detail in her books.

Holly North has written four other Doctor Nurse Romances, *A Surgeon Surrenders*, *Sister Slater's Secret*, *Nurse at Large* and *Dr Malone, I Presume?* to which this book is a sequel.

THE INVISIBLE DOCTOR

BY

HOLLY NORTH

MILLS & BOON LIMITED
ETON HOUSE 18–24 PARADISE ROAD
RICHMOND SURREY TW9 1SR

*First published in Great Britain 1987
by Mills & Boon Limited*

© Holly North 1987

*Australian copyright 1987
Philippine copyright 1987*

ISBN 0 263 75909 1

*Set in 11 on 12½ pt. Linotron Times
03–1187–44050*

*Made and printed in Great Britain by
Collins, Glasgow*

CHAPTER ONE

HANGING the keys to the medicine trolley on the hook behind her desk, where Sister Parker had always kept them, Nina suddenly caught a glimpse of herself in the mirror, also Sister Parker's, which was placed discreetly by the side of the filing cabinet. It enabled the occupant of the desk to check herself before she went out on to the ward or received a visitor, but its position, out of sight of anyone entering the room, confounded any talk of vanity. Sister Parker was clever when it came to things like that—clever at everything, in fact. That was why she'd gone to join the hierarchy of SNO's and DNO's who ran the entire area's hospitals. And *that* was why Nina was sitting here in her old office and running the ward she'd worked on for more than three years.

She stole another glance at the silver-grey uniform that singled her out from her fellow nurses in their lilac and white stripes. To be honest, the colour didn't do much for her colouring. But it felt good just to see herself in a Sister's uniform, even if at the moment she was in the role of Acting Sister. They'd put her on a three-month probationary period to see how she got on with running the ward, explaining that she didn't technically have the experience behind her. But Sister Parker had recommended her, and everything Sister Parker said and did was taken seriously.

Nina turned her attention to the piles of paperwork sitting on her desk. Of course she'd known that in a modern hospital the rôle of Sister was as much one involved with administration as nursing, and Sister Parker had trained her carefully in the month before she had left the ward, but even so the sheer day-to-day bulk of it hadn't hit her until she'd found herself on her own during her first week. Look at it now—a whole batch of patients' records to go through and check before sending them back down to the records department, and on top of that a whole pile of memos, reports and minutes of meetings which she'd have to read before going to the next one. She might as well start it now, she reasoned, picking up the top sheet. It contained a report on an internal study done in the hospital on standards of hygiene, and it made fascinating reading. The report's compilers had come to the conclusion that thirty per cent of Moorside patients were cross-infected during their stay; that while being treated for one condition they caught another, which slowed up their recovery and took up valuable beds. There would be a symposium to discuss the various findings, and Sisters were asked to attend, it concluded. Nina dutifully made a note of it in her diary and vowed to do some homework on the subject so that she and her nurses wouldn't be shown up.

Lab reports came next, and she checked them and attached them to patients' files so that when the doctors came to do their rounds they had a copy on hand. An hour passed in phone calls and signing letters, and as the minutes ticked by Nina's natural enthusiasm began to wane. She'd never get to the bottom of it! Perhaps, a private doubt intruded, she shouldn't have put herself up for the job in the first place. Stuck behind this desk for hours every day, she didn't even have the pleasure of getting to know the patients and watching them get better gradually. Of course she did her tour of the ward twice a day, checking that everyone was all right, but then it was straight back behind her desk and on with the paperwork and the meetings and the phone calls . . .

'Nina! Sorry, I keep forgetting, *Sister!* Would you come along to the kitchen, please?' Helen Osborne, her trusty staff nurse, stood bristling in the doorway. 'Mr Barratt's been at it again, and he's managed to upset one of the new students. She won't stop crying for me, and now the others are getting stroppy. You'd better come and calm the mutiny while you can.'

'What's he done now?' Nina looked despairingly down at the notes she was in the middle of updating. Mr Barratt had been a nuisance from the day he'd arrived, calling lewd comments across the ward and badgering everyone with offensive suggestions. First the cleaning supervisor had been along to complain. Then a night nurse had protested that he'd slapped her bottom after calling her over to his bed. His hernia repair operation had slowed him up for a day or two, although he'd managed to offend the anaesthetist by passing comment on the size of his assistant's bosom just before he drifted off to sleep, but now he was feeling better and getting more disagreeable by the minute.

'Not much more than he's been doing since the day he arrived—pinching your bottom the minute you turn your back on him,' Helen said ruefully.

'Not you too?' asked Nina, unable to keep the smile from her face. 'You were the one who was telling the students not to turn their backs on him, I seem to remember.'

'It's not funny.' Helen was obviously not amused, and her grim look sobered Nina. 'You don't have to put up with it in here, maybe, but it's horrible for the rest of us. I went to give him a sponge bath yesterday and he whispered some obscene proposition in my ear. Then I had to strip him down and wash him just as if nothing had happened.'

'I'll get him off the ward.' The promise was out before Nina had had time to think it through. It was obvious, from what Helen said, that she hadn't been as sensitive to feelings on the ward as she should have been. Nina knew she should have done something about it when Mr Barratt had first arrived, but here she was, new to her position of authority and unwilling to throw her weight about too much. And what made it worse was that Mr Barratt's surgeon was new to the hospital himself, and playing the game very much by the book.

Another surgeon might have discharged his patient at the earliest opportunity, but Mr Farris wasn't going to take any risks during his first weeks here. Nina picked up the phone. 'I'll call Mr Farris now and ask him to discharge Mr Barratt. We really can't be expected to put up with this.'

'You haven't heard the worst yet,' said Helen. 'From what I can get out of Kate, he put his hand down the front of her uniform——'

'That really is too much! Honestly, it's not as if we didn't have enough to cope with,' Nina fumed. 'I promise you, Helen, he'll be out of here by tonight.'

'Good.' Helen turned on her heel and left Nina waiting for someone to answer the phone down in the surgeons' sitting-room. As the phone rang and rang, she felt her blood coming slowly to the boil. It was odd how things could infuriate her so quickly, but she had inherited a volatile temper from her mother, who was half Italian. You only had to look at her, actually, to realise that she was one of those people who had a short fuse. Acting Sister Newington was a small, dark spitfire of a nurse. Under the fluorescent tubes of her ward when she did a round early in the morning or late in the evening her dark hair gleamed blue-black. And when she was angry, sometimes even before she knew she was angry, her fine dark eyebrows would descend in a threatening line across her forehead. It was an early-warning sign for the people around her. Helen had just noticed it, and with a smile she returned to the nurses' kitchen. 'It's all right,' she told the three students who stood in a knot around their friend, who was sobbing at the table. 'Sister's going to sort him out.'

Having finally got through to the surgeons' sitting-room, only to discover that Mr Farris was still in Theatre, Nina made her own way to the kitchen. The student nurses, all looking ridiculously young and nervous, and all slightly too small for their uniforms, turned expectantly towards her, which threw her off her stride for a moment. But by now her temper was flaring. She wanted to hear the worst, then go and confront the troublemaker with it.

'I hear you've had a problem with Mr Barratt,' Kate. Tell me what happened, would you?'

'He's a pervert, Sister!' burst out one of the other students.

Nina glanced at her sternly. 'I shall make up my own mind about that. Kate, your story, please.'

'I was just doing a blood pressure check on him—Nurse Osborne told me to,' Kate Hardy explained. 'When I'd finished he complained of a sharp pain in his shoulderblade and asked if I'd take a look at it. He bent forward so that I could take a look down the back of his pyjama jacket, and the next thing I knew he'd somehow put his hand down the front of my uniform . . .' She sniffed again. 'I'm sorry to be such a wet, Sister, but I don't think I can bear much more of this. I thought people were supposed to respect nurses.'

'There are some men who don't respect any

women at all,' Nina said archly. 'Come on, Kate, these things tend to happen to pretty young nurses like you. I've been nursing for nine years now and I've never met anyone like Mr Barratt before. Once we've got rid of him you'll begin to enjoy yourself again.' Her thoughts flew back to a lecture she had attended as part of a Women's Studies group she'd joined a year or two ago. 'Men have lots of silly ideas about women in positions of power—nurses and traffic wardens,' she smiled. Kate laughed and wiped her eyes. 'It's the result of all those years of *Carry On* films, where nurses were just silly bits of fluff for the doctors to play with.'

'Mr Barratt seems to think that we should be wearing black stockings and suspenders,' said another student. 'At least, that's what he told me when he goosed me yesterday.'

'Just let me get my hands on him!' Nina meant it laughingly, but her disgust and anger were evident. 'I've called Mr Farris and I hope that in an hour or two we can wave goodbye to Mr Barratt. In the meantime, I shall go and have a word with him myself. Kate, you go and take half an hour's break. Go and have a cup of tea in the canteen. Jane, you can go with her. The rest of you had better get back to what you were doing before this happened. You're supposed to be here to learn, you know, not to stand gossiping in the kitchen.'

As Nina strode out of the kitchen and turned into the ward, her brows beetling, one of the students turned to the others. 'Poor Mr Barratt, I almost feel sorry for him,' she grinned. 'He won't know what's hit him! He's probably chosen the worst person in the whole hospital to annoy.'

'Why's that?' asked Kate.

'Sister's a feminist. I was speaking to one of the junior housemen over lunch'—the others looked impressed—'and he said that she's very into women's rights. Apparently she goes to assertiveness training courses and women's groups, so she won't put up with this.'

'Well, I hope she gives him what for,' Kate said ruefully.

'I bet she will!'

James Farris turned right as he emerged from the surgeons' sitting-room, then remembered that he was no longer at Highstead Hospital in London and retraced his steps, found the lift, climbed in amid two coyly smiling physiotherapists and an old gentleman carrying a huge bunch of sweet peas and gazed selfconsciously at the floor indicator. He'd forgotten how uncomfortable it could be, being the new boy. For a start, after so long at Highstead he was finding it difficult to get his bearings here. He was for ever turning in the wrong direction, getting hopelessly lost and having to ask patients for directions. Then there was the friendliness of people here. After years of living in London, where you could have worked with people for years but never said much more than 'Good morning' and 'Good night' to them, he'd got out of the habit of chatting to staff and patients alike. And he was painfully aware that for this reason some of them had already decided he was standoffish. For a minute, as he walked along the white-tiled corridor to Men's Surgical, he wondered whether he'd done the right thing in moving back up here. After all, just because he'd been born in Yorkshire and spent his childhood here it didn't mean that it was the place for him.

He thought back over the last few months—of Abby, whom he'd been so sure he'd marry and spend the rest of his life with, and Sam, the best friend who had come back and claimed her. Then there had been his own worrying illness, which had proved to him how precarious his career was and how much he liked working with people. The shock of the two events together had made him think hard about his life and the way he wanted to live. London hadn't seemed to hold much pleasure for him any more, so when he had heard about this job he had jumped at the chance to make a clean break.

He paused at a window which looked out over the surrounding roofs to the Yorkshire moors. Here, not far from York, he had the best of all worlds—beautiful scenery for walking and relaxing in, and a lively and interesting city for evenings and weekends. It was, he knew in his heart, a good decision. It wouldn't be long before he felt that he'd been fully absorbed into hospital life. It wouldn't take long for him to make himself known. And maybe, with a bit of luck, he would find someone to replace Abby. He sighed as he thought about her.

He couldn't banish her from his thoughts, no matter what he did. His first instinct had been to vow never to get involved with a nurse again. They were too worldly-wise; they had to be down-to-earth and determined for them to enjoy their jobs. But he liked them because they were caring and dedicated, and because they knew the realities of a surgeon's job. Other women seemed to expect him to be Dr Kildare all the time, and weren't impressed if he was so tired after four nights' surgery in a row that he fell asleep in the cinema or refused to go to a party. At least a nurse knew what to expect when she got involved with a doctor.

With difficulty James dragged himself back from the view and his daydreams. It was just gone five and visitors were being put out of the wards. Moorside was a liberal hospital with an open-hours policy when it came to visiting, but it *did* shut its ward doors between the hours of five and six so that dinners could be served. He supposed he should go immediately to Men's Surgical to see Sister Newington, but he didn't relish the prospect. Two days after he had first arrived he had been invited to a party by another surgeon. They had gone along, and James had met a vast number of Moorside staff, including Nina. At first he had seen her across the room and been taken by the animation and brightness in her eyes and looks. She wasn't one of those languid, pale girls who pouted invitingly—in fact she had seemed to be involved in an argument with one of the other doctors. James had admired her upright, direct stance and her very short, dark hair that gave her a boyish look. She was exactly the opposite of Abby, who had been tall with wonderful waist-length blonde hair. Alone and in a new job, miles from the people and places that he knew, James had on the instant decided that Nina Newington—for that, his companion had told him, was her name—might be worth getting to know. He'd wondered why Andrew Hartley had laughed so loud when he had expressed his interest in Nina. Then he met her and understood why.

Within five minutes of being introduced, he had found himself pitted in argument with her. Some innocuous little comment he had made about the people in this part of the country being more friendly than those in the south had aroused her ire. He couldn't for the life of him remember exactly how the argument had gone, simply that everything he said had been turned on him, and in ten minutes he had been completely flattened by her. She had left him with a brusque handshake, a victorious smile and the hope that they would meet and continue their discussion some time.

James had had to have a strong drink to recover. 'It's all right,' Andrew Hartley had chortled,' she's like that with all the men. She's a real Women's Libber, Nina—believes it's the women of the world who make it go round and that we men just get in the way. But you should have seen your face!' He laughed again.

Since then, fortunately, James had managed to avoid having any more 'discussions' with her. On his trip to the ward he was normally accompanied either by students—because this, unlike High-stead, was a training hospital—or by another surgeon. Anyway, most of the time he was in and out quickly, doing pre- and post-operative checks. Nina had recently been put in charge of the ward on a three-month probationary period and was pre-sumably too busy to pick fights with surgeons. Even so, James's heart fell when he looked again at the scrawled message that had been handed to him as he'd walked into the surgeons' sitting-room. It was about Mr Barratt. And he had a horrible feeling that Mr Barratt was a subject on which he and Sister Nina Newington were not going to agree.

'Mr Barratt, I don't think you quite realise how serious the situation is.' Nina held her hands behind her back. What she'd really like to do to this overweight Lothario was give him a great clip around the ear, something that he wouldn't be able to forget.

He just laughed. 'I can't understand all the fuss, lass. It was just a bit of a joke, that's all. What do you expect a man to do, surrounding him with all these pretty little nurses? Most of them look as if they've just left school! If they can't take it in the spirit in which it was intended then that's their look-out . . .'

Nina wondered what they did to nurses who grievously injured their patients in the line of duty. But what good would clouting him do? He simply seemed unable to understand that his behaviour was profoundly offensive. 'You have sexually assaulted one of my nurses,' she ground out, 'and now you're telling me it's her fault! It's gone beyond the stage of patting us on the bottom as we pass by, you know. In fact if I cared to call the police I'm sure they'd take the complaint very seriously.'

'Get lost!' Mr Barratt waved his arm dismissively at her. 'Nurses, police, you're all bloody bureaucrats. Who do you think you are? You can't be a day over twenty-five—what do you think you're doing, telling a man like me what I should think and do?'

Nina's lips tightened. Where were the good old days, when a nurse's uniform had been enough to ensure her safety and respect in even the roughest areas? She looked back on her own days in training, not a decade ago, when taxi drivers had refused to take her fare and courteous middle-aged men, glimpsing her uniform as she'd walked back to the nurses' home at night, had walked alongside with nothing in their minds except seeing her safely to her door. Now, almost every week the nursing papers reported more moves in hospitals to make the staff safe; screens in A&E, security guards in reception areas, policemen patrolling Outpatients —and now she had a patient threatening nurses on the ward.

'There's another thing I want to raise with you, *Sister*,' he said sneeringly. 'I've noticed that I'm the last one to be served every mealtime, which means my dinner's usually cold by the time it gets here. I'm surprised you haven't noticed it and done something about it. And there's something else too.' He stabbed a finger at her accusingly. 'I've noticed that a lot of the other patients get a bath every day if they ask for it. I've been asking and I'm always told they're too busy or that I'm not to have a bath today. What do you say about that, eh?'

'I'd say, Mr Barratt, that nurses are human. Someone in this ward has to be served last at mealtimes. And we're often too busy to give all the patients who would like one a proper bath every day. If the nurses like you and you make yourself pleasant to them you'll find that they try to make your life as easy and comfortable as possible. But if you assault them and insult them you can't expect them to put themselves out for you.'

'It's not fair! It's not bloody fair!' he cried. 'In fact I've a good mind to report you and your nurses, Sister. You're not looking after me properly—it's obvious. I had my hernia done the same day as the chap in the next bed and he went home on Thursday. You're ignoring my treatment, that's what you're doing.'

Nina's eyes blazed fire. 'I've got news for you. You're going home just as soon as I can get a surgeon in here to release you. I warn you, Mr Barratt, you're not spending another night on this ward. I've had to speak to you three times already about harassing my staff, and you've continued to make a nuisance of yourself. Well, I'm not going to stand for it any more!' It was too late now. She couldn't stop herself, he was looking at her with such a horrible, smug grin. In fact he wasn't even looking at her, because his eyes kept moving over her shoulder, doubtless watching a nurse passing beyond the bed curtains. 'You're a lout, Mr Barratt, and this ward will be a happier place when you're gone. And you're going today!'

'I think perhaps I'd better be the judge of that, Sister.' James wished he didn't have to do it, but he did. He'd been standing there listening for a whole minute, waiting for a chance to announce himself. He felt Nina's basilisk gaze turn on him and wondered why, although she terrified him, he also felt that her opinion of him mattered.

'Mr Farris—I'm sorry, I didn't realise you were here,' she said crisply. How fortunate it was that she didn't blush! If she'd been inclined to blushing she would have been pink from her forehead to her knees by now. As it was, the tips of her ears burned brightly, but she seemed to keep her composure. 'Mr Barratt would very much like to leave the hospital—and I and the rest of my staff would also be grateful if you felt able to discharge him.'

'I'm sure you'll all appreciate that it's not a matter of *wanting* to go,' James said formally, embarrassed at being stuck in the middle of an unhappy situation. 'I'll certainly carry out an examination, though, and if Mr Barratt is fit enough to be discharged I'll be happy to let him go.' He waited for her reaction and tried not to flinch as her furious gaze travelled up and down his smart double-breasted grey suit and his muscular frame. James Farris wasn't perhaps the best-looking member of the medical staff at Moorside, but he had an open, friendly, almost boyish countenance that spoke of honesty and reliability and good health. A lot of doctors could be dismissed as pompous or arrogant or difficult, but he was none of these. In fact Nina had rather liked him when they'd first met at that party. If only she hadn't just had a furious row with one of the junior housemen, they might have hit it off. Unfortunately she had been in such a blazing temper that the moment James had told her he'd just come up to Moorside from London, and added some little remark about people in the north being less sophisticated than in the south, she'd let rip at him. And not being one much given to apologising, she was aware that she had at one blow ruined whatever there might have been between them.

For his part, James didn't understand why Sister Newington had got it in for him—but she had, there was no doubt about that, and his only way of keeping things on an even keel was to pull rank with her. From what he'd seen she was a competent and conscientious nurse. She seemed to spend a great deal of extra time on the ward, and he'd seen her teaching her students in an understanding and capable manner. She seemed to get on with all the other women on the ward very well. It was just men—and here he felt fraternal sympathy with Mr Barratt, loathsome man as he was—she seemed to have a problem with.

'I'll just examine him, shall I?' James stepped out of the cubicle and went to scrub his hands at the basin. Meanwhile, Nina sent one of the students to bring the dressings trolley and, with James looking on, gingerly rolled back Mr Barratt's bedclothes, exposed the operation site, and used the dressings forceps to lift the gauze away.

'It looks very nice, though I say so myself,' James commented, pressing the area around the stitches and casually watching the patient's face for any sign of pain. There was none. 'It's a very clean wound, Sister. I congratulate you.' He smiled across Mr Barratt's flaccid white belly. Nina did not smile back, even though she felt pleased that he had acknowledged the care with which his patient had been treated. 'Perhaps you could ask one of your staff nurses to come and replace the dressing while we have a word,' James suggested gamely, trying to ignore the irritation that was building up in him.

Nina left the cubicle to call Helen, who came over wearily. 'Would you replace Mr Barratt's dressing, please,' she requested. 'Take one of the students with you, so they can watch. You might even let her have a go herself, come to think of it. And if he touches or pinches you in any way, yell and I'll come running.'

'I might just accidentally stab him with the forceps,' Helen said grimly, motioning to one of the students who was carrying flowers in vases up the ward. 'Jane, when you've put those down I'd like you to come and give me a hand.'

Nina walked back to the basin just a few feet down from Mr Barratt's bed, where James was scrupulously washing his hands. She held out one of the freshly-laundered towels for him and he took it silently. 'Well?' she asked.

'Perhaps we could have a word in your office?' he suggested, and wondered why he felt like a naughty schoolboy offering to turn himself in to his head-master.

The march up the ward was a long, slow one. The other nursing staff turned and watched expectantly as Nina and the new consultant passed by. 'Don't say he's going to refuse to let Mr Barratt go home!' muttered Kate Hardy to the nursing auxiliary with whom she was making a bed. And those were the very words that Nina uttered the moment she had shut the door of her office.

'Don't tell me you're not going to discharge him!' she said with quiet fury. 'He has no pain, the wound is healing perfectly, he's got a wife to look after him at home . . .'

'It's not that easy,' protested James, 'and to be perfectly frank, Sister, I think you should be content to let me be the judge in these matters. I'd like him to stay for two more days, that's all, so that we can be certain that he's completely recovered.'

Nina's brows beetled to form a fine black line above her eyes, which shot warning sparks. 'Mr Farris, I think you're being unnecessarily cautious! Mr Hartley and Mr Sellers would both have dis-charged him last week. I know you want to be careful, but I must draw to your attention to the fact that my staff are no longer willing to nurse Mr Barratt. And as he no longer needs specialised nursing the obvious thing to do is to send him home.'

James was rarely roused to anger. Although he was sandy-haired he was the kind of mild and equable man who could get on with almost anyone. But this! He had never been spoken to in such a way before, and certainly not by some upstart of a Sister who had a personal grudge against his patient. 'What Mr Hartley or Mr Sellers would do in this situation is nothing to do with either you or me, Sister Newington,' he said sharply. 'When it comes to decisions about Mr Barratt *I* make them and you carry them out. I hope we both understand that.'

'In which case I shall call Administration and make a formal complaint about his behaviour on this ward,' Nina retorted. 'And I shall make a particular point of the fact that you've done nothing to help us in this matter. You've just washed your hands of the whole thing!'

'Now look!' James banged his hand so hard on the table that a pile of paperwork slipped dramatically to the floor, surprising him. It had been years since he had done anything so aggressive, and he found himself wondering what it was about this woman that made him want to blow his top. 'Mr Barratt is a handful, I know. But the fact that he's a pest . . .'

'A pest!' Nina threw her hands in the air in utter disgust. 'A pest? Is that what you call a man who can scarcely manage a sentence without innuendo or sexual comments? He's humiliated my nurses, the cleaning staff, the night staff, the anaesthetist —and you just call him a pest! The man's a pervert, a maniac!'

James stood back and was silent for a few moments. She had got the whole thing out of proportion, blown it all up and made it far more serious than it really was. Any minute now she would realise how ridiculous she sounded and come back down to earth.

He shrugged, a move that made her blood seethe all the more. 'Surely,' he said patiently, 'your staff can put up with one awkward patient for just two days more? Is that really too much to ask? It doesn't reflect awfully, well on you, Sister, if you can't cope with one bedridden sex fiend for another forty-eight hours.'

Nina couldn't believe what she was hearing. 'Are you trying to imply that it's my fault that he's managed to wreak such havoc?' she asked incredulously.

'No,' he smiled equably, unaware of the wrath that was about to fall on his head. 'But if you'd handled the situation a little more calmly, perhaps, and played down its importance, your staff wouldn't have become quite as upset as they obviously are. This kind of thing happens in all hospitals, but it's not the end of the world. Men are men, Sister, and just because you don't happen to like the way they think and behave, you can't deprive them of the medical care they deserve.'

The strangled noise that rose from Nina's throat was a roar of fury. 'Mr Farris, you're the most unabashed, outrageous male chauvinist pig I've had the misfortune to meet in my entire career!' Her voice was low with seething ire and she waved a finger under his nose, quite without thought for what her actions might lead to. It had gone beyond a problem of an awkward patient making life difficult on the ward. Now it was a matter of principle. 'We have twenty-eight patients to care for on this ward and one of them, *your* patient, is making daily procedure intolerable for us. Not for me, I should point out, but for my junior staff and students. The cleaning staff have already reported an incident to their union, and I've warned Mr Barratt on their behalf. The night staff have registered a complaint and I've warned him about that too. Now he's got to the stage where he's assaulting my nurses, and you won't do anything about it!'

'I'll warn him myself,' James butted in. 'I'll make it quite clear that this kind of behaviour can't go on.'

'Do you honestly think he'll take any more notice of me than of you?' asked Nina witheringly.

'Yes,' James replied, adding, without thought, 'a warning from a male surgeon will have more effect than a warning from a woman, whatever her rank.' It was the wrong thing, and he knew it immediately by the flash of pure hatred that leapt from Nina's eyes. 'Oh God,' he protested, putting up his hand in defence, 'look, I didn't mean it like that!'

'Oh yes, you did, Mr Farris!' She practically spat the words at him. 'What you mean is that because I'm a woman I shouldn't expect to be taken too seriously on this ward. The fact that I'm in charge of it means nothing to you, does it? What I really need, as a nurse in a position of authority, is your support. What I need you to say is that this situation can't go on—and you should prove it to Mr Barratt by discharging him this afternoon. Instead of which you're siding with him against me. And it goes further than that—it has a political dimension——'

'There's no need to lecture me on loony feminist politics,' James inserted quickly, immediately hating himself for saying it. He *did* support women's rights. Abby had been pretty liberated, and he had always supported her. He didn't like dependent women, women who replied on him for everything, so what was he doing, sounding like the male chauvinist pig Nina had accused him of being? 'Look, I didn't mean that either,' he added, shaking his head despairingly.

'Oh, didn't you?' Nina retorted disbelievingly. 'Then prove that you support the nurses by going out there and discharging Mr Barratt.'

'I can't do that,' James sighed helplessly. 'As a surgeon, I just can't do it, and as a nurse you shouldn't be encouraging me to.'

'Do you realise what you're doing with this decision?' she asked, glaring at him. 'You're telling all the men out there that they have the right to behave to us just as they think fit. You're saying to them that they don't have to take any notice of us—they can treat us as insultingly as they like and they'll still get let off with a smacked hand and a warning not to do it again. It's that attitude that's leading to nurses getting attacked in hospitals—and because no one takes our grievances seriously we're not paid properly either . . .'

'I don't have time to discuss nurses' pay,' James intercepted neatly. 'You can say whatever you like, Sister, but I'm going to give Mr Barratt a stiff talking-to and a final warning. I'll be back to see him and you the day after tomorrow. And that's the end of it.' And with that he swept out, slamming the office door behind him and striding down the ward to where Mr Barratt lay, just a trifle nervously, in his bed.

Nina didn't hear what ensued, deeming it better to stay in the sanctuary of her own office. Her cheeks burned with invisible heat and a headache began to throb behind her temples. What was worse, a quiet dread of what she had said to James Farris had begun to consume her. She had got carried away, and in doing so she had ruined her own argument. She cursed herself for not being more level-headed. Why couldn't she appeal to people on a calmer level? Why did her temper suddenly snap like that? She heard his distinctive footsteps pass her door as he made his way out of the ward, and dared to open the door.

Helen Osborne stood grinning from ear to ear outside. 'I don't know what you said to him, Nina —sorry, Sister—but Mr Farris just gave Mr Barratt a real roasting!'

'Did he?' said Nina coolly, with a touch of disbelief.

'He threatened to prosecute if he tries anything

on again, and worse too. It's nice to know he's on our side, isn't it?'

Nina just gritted her teeth.

CHAPTER TWO

'WELL, this is it.' The estate agent led Nina into the hallway of the house. It was attractive, built of mellowed grey stone with large white-framed windows. 'Hmm,' he mumbled, drawing her back from the large panelled door that led into the ground floor apartment. 'I'm afraid the flat *you've* come to look at is upstairs, Miss Newington.' Something about his tone of voice managed to imply that she would never be able to afford the more spacious conversion, and she bridled. Ever since she had begun looking for a place of her own, she had come up against the condescension of estate agents and bank managers alike. They didn't seem willing to believe that a woman on her own could afford to buy a flat, however basic and rock-bottom its price. All the other people on the market seemed to be young couples; a woman on her own seemed a rarity. She held her chin high and followed the estate agent up the stairs. She'd show them—bank managers, estate agents, the lot of them—that nothing could stop a woman with determination. And James Farris too. She'd get even with him, just see if she didn't!

The flat was up two flights of stairs which grew progressively narrower at the top. The agent paused, panting hard, and wiped his brow, slightly

embarrassed by the crumpled state of his handkerchief. 'The bottom flat occupies the first two floors,
and of course, it has the garden. The flat we're
going to see has been converted from the attic,' he
explained. 'That's why it's so . . . er . . . reasonable.' He stuffed his handkerchief back in his
pocket and resumed the climb. Nina frowned. He
had made it quite clear that it was a cheap flat. She
finished the climb behind him, and was pleased that
it had scarcely raised her pulse rate. The estate
agent might have money but at least she was fit and
healthy, even after a hard day's work on the ward.

'This is the hall . . .' He flung the door open
wide, as if he was showing her around a palace. It
gave on to a small square hall with four doors
leading off. 'The bathroom.' Nina glimpsed a pink
bath and a big dormer window looking out on to
gardens and, in the distance, the hazy greys and
purples of the moors. 'Sitting-room.' A smallish
white-painted room with another dormer window
with a similar view. 'Kitchen.' It was very cramped,
just enough room to swing a kitten, but there were
neat white units trimmed with red handles, which
she immediately warmed to. Red was her favourite
colour—red and green, anyway. With her vivid
colouring she could get away with strong shades.
She was wearing a vibrant emerald green sweater
today, over loose-fitting charcoal and white striped
trousers. The estate agent looked at her admiringly
as she walked over to the window and tried the
catches. She had a slightly foreign look in the way
she dressed, and her dark eyes and hair reminded

him of an Italian girl he had met many years ago . . .

'Well, this window doesn't open, for a start,' said Nina matter-of-factly, shattering his reminiscences. 'How about the wiring?'

'All new,' he hastened to assure her. 'The central heating is new too—all put in by the man who owns the house.'

'This radiator's got a leak,' noticed his client, indicating with the toe of her white leather baseball-style boots the stained hardboard that covered the floor. 'And there aren't enough electric points.' The estate agent gave her a telling look that seemed to reproach her for not being grateful. 'Who lives downstairs?' she asked curiously.

'The man who owns the house,' he replied. 'He doesn't need the space up here, so he had it converted and now he's selling it on a lease. You're lucky to have seen it, really. It's a very good area and I've got a dozen other clients who are looking for something just like this.'

Nina couldn't help but agree with him, though she wouldn't admit it. 'It's very small, though,' she protested, opening the bedroom door and sticking her head around. This room was bigger than the others, with two windows looking out over the road that ran in front of the house. There was a large built-in cupboard on either side of the chimney breast, which still contained its original cast-iron fireplace. 'This is nice, though.' She stood in the centre of the room and turned slowly round, inspecting the plasterwork, looking for telltale signs of damp. She'd had enough practice; she'd been looking for a flat for the last four months. And despite all its drawbacks, this was the best she had yet seen. 'How much did you say it was?' she asked casually.

The estate agent named some exorbitant sum, three times her salary as a Sister. Nina tried to look aghast, but couldn't manage it. She was home, and she knew it. Already she could see her possessions scattered about the place. She could see the exact spots to hang her posters and paintings. She knew instinctively that she could make the kitchen homely and the bathroom welcoming, despite its wishy-washy pink bath. 'I'll buy it,' she stated flatly. 'Subject to a survey, of course.'

Suddenly the estate agent looked pale. 'You *have* considered the disadvantages?' he questioned. 'All those stairs, for example. And up here under the roof . . .'

Nina hardly heard him. She was quite aware that she would curse the stairs every evening when she came dragging in from a long day on the ward. She knew that here, at the top of the house, her heating bills would be higher and stormy nights noisier than if she'd settled for a basement flat. But from up here she could see right to the distant horizon, over gardens and then out to the countryside beyond. It was like living up in an eyrie, away from all the noise and bustle of the world. What were a few problems with windows that didn't open and leaking radiators? Nowhere was going to be perfect, at least not for the price that she could afford.

'There's just one thing,' she asked hesitantly. 'What about the man downstairs? He's not some hairy lout who's going to play heavy metal music all night, is he? And he's not a middle-aged fatherly type who'll want to know where I'm going every time I leave the house?'

'He's a very nice young man, a professional, I believe,' reassured the estate agent, anxious now to complete the deal. 'He hasn't lived here long himself, from what I gather. He told me that this flat was let to students when he first moved in, but he didn't want any headbangers, I believe that's what he called them, living above him, so he'd done it up to sell to someone suitable.'

'And do you think he'll think *I'm* suitable?' asked Nina. To her the man downstairs sounded like a real stick-in-the mud.

The estate agent looked taken aback. 'Oh, yes, I should think so. And you never know,' he added with a sly glance. 'As far as I know there isn't a lady living downstairs . . .'

Nina darted him a dismissive look. 'I have twenty-eight men in my life already—there's certainly not enough room for even *one* more.' The estate agent looked confused. 'I have twenty-eight demanding male patients on my ward,' she explained patiently.

'Ah.' They stood viewing the flat in silence for another minute. It *was* small; it *was*, in many ways, inconvenient; it was not what she had originally set out to buy. But it was homely, and she could picture herself living here, with her friends coming round for Sunday lunch and her parents staying for the weekend.

'Well,' she suggested, shutting the kitchen door with a firm click, 'hadn't we better go back to the office, so that I can put a deposit down on this place and we can get the ball rolling?' She smiled to herself as she descended the stairs with their beige cord carpeting. She was going to be a woman of property!

It was Tuesday afternoon, and at two p.m. each Tuesday the Moorside Sisters met in the conference room on the third floor of the hospital. Even though she was still only an Acting Sister, Nina went along too. She sat at the long table and noted, for the dozenth time, how the Sisters split pretty evenly into nursing staff of the old and new schools. About half of them, many in the most senior positions and most of them unmarried, were in their forties and fifties, and generally they had a traditional outlook. Increasingly, though, they were being joined by much younger women, many of them determined to make a good career for themselves and to improve the lot of nurses in general. It made for lively meetings, particularly when cuts in Health Service spending were discussed or there were issues over staff pay. Some of the older Sisters tended to the view that nurses went into the profession knowing that it was poorly paid, and that they should accept things as they were. Many of the younger ones felt differently, arguing that they and their nurses had come into nursing

because they wanted to nurse, and that the fact that
nursing had always been a low-paid profession
didn't mean that it should be a low-paid profession
for ever. They pointed out that nurses had to train
for years and that their jobs were becoming
increasingly complex and skilled as medicine
advanced. Although Sisters' meetings were always
well-behaved, these kind of issues raised the
temperature of the occasion no end. Today, fortunately, things had been very routine.

'Our final item on the agenda,' announced the
SNO, 'is our wedding present for Mr Sturgis, the
urological consultant. After our collection last
week Sister Gifford has bought this attractive
tablecloth and napkin set.' She waved the gift for all
to see. 'If you'd all please sign this card for him, I'll
present it on Thursday.' A wedding card, all pink
and silver and bows and hearts, was passed down
the table. It wasn't the kind of thing Nina would
have chosen herself, but she duly signed and passed
the card on. It was a tradition at Moorside that
senior nursing staff gave an individual gift to
medical and surgical staff. Just one more of the
little details involved in being a Sister. 'Any other
business?' asked the SNO, as everyone began to
fold away their agendas and pick up their notes.

'Yes,' chirped Angie Sinclair from the very end
of the table. 'I don't know if any of you have
noticed, but a new cinema has opened on the
corner of the High Street and the York Road.'

'Yes, I *have*,' sniffed Sister Hallwell, who was
coming up for retirement after running the Gynae

ward for nearly thirty years. 'I don't think it's
the kind of thing we should discuss here, Sister
Sinclair.'

Angie Sinclair and Phyllis Hallwell did not like
each other. Sister Hallwell was a traditionalist of
the old school who believed that nurses were put
into the world to suffer all the slings and arrows that
patients, the Health Service and their seniors could
throw at them. When Nina remembered her time
on Gynae it was with a little shudder of relief that
she had managed to escape. Angie Sinclair, who
had been only a year ahead of her in training
school, was a star in everything she did. She had
passed highest in all her exams, she had been the
best-looking and brightest of a whole generation of
Moorside students. And not only had she married
good-looking Tim Sinclair, the most eligible doctor
in the hospital, but she had become the youngest
Sister on record when she was promoted to that
position nearly two years ago. She ran the children's ward with a combination of the old values
and some very new and radical ideas, which startled
and unsettled some of the traditionalists on the
staff. Angie it was who had fought the administra-
tors and the powers-that-be to get a special room
put aside for parents to stay overnight with their
children. It was Angie who had held out a long feud
with the catering staff and nutritionists until at last
it was agreed that the children in her care could eat
in hospital the kind of food they really enjoyed
—not roasts and pasta and curry, but beefburgers
and beans and chips. After all, she had argued, if

they ate nothing at all, or unwillingly, they were unlikely to recover as quickly as if they were eating normally. The idea of chips with everything sent a shudder down the spine of Phyllis Hallwell, but the popularity of the move with everyone had ensured that it was here to stay.

Now Angie ignored her rival's remark. 'For those of you who don't have to pass it on the way to work perhaps I should explain that it's a blue movie cinema. And among the films it's got lined up this week are—' she paused and consulted the sheet of paper she had taken from her file '—*Secrets of the Naughty Night Nurses, Nurse Knows Best* and *Off Duty Doctor*. I won't go into details, but the whole front of the building is plastered with pictures of topless nurses in black suspenders. I really think we ought to do something about it.'

'So do I!' It came out quite spontaneously, and Nina heard herself saying confidently, 'Only last week I had a patient who made a constant sexual nuisance of himself throughout his stay on the ward. He'd obviously seen this kind of film. And I should add,' she went on hotly, 'that when I approached his surgeon about the problem I was told that it was just high spirits and that I and my staff were being paranoid about it.'

'Exactly,' Angie said approvingly. 'These films are damaging nurses' chances of being taken seriously. They totally distort what nurses do and encourage men to treat us in a sexist way.'

Phyllis Hallwell tapped her pencil on the desk and said in a voice full of mock amusement, 'Well,

I'm sure that I and the other *senior* staff here never have any trouble with sexual harassment on *our* wards! We'd know how to deal with such things if they arose. What exactly do you propose to do about this cinema, Sister Sinclair?'

Both Nina and Angie bridled visibly. The meaning of Sister Hallwell's words was quite clear, as was her knowing look to the other like-minded staff round the table. What she was saying was that if such young and inexperienced staff were going to be promoted to positions of authority, what did the others expect?

'I think we should organise a picket of the place, with placards and as many nurses as we can muster. That should get plenty of coverage in the local papers and perhaps even on television, and then we could make our point about nurses being ordinary, hard-working women. We'll have to act quickly, though, because they change the films each week.'

'We could do it on Friday,' mused Nina. 'And I'm sure that several nurses from Men's Surgical would turn out after their recent experience.'

'It all sounds a little extreme,' inserted the SNO, trying, as always, to mediate between the two opposing camps. 'Couldn't we just write a letter to the owners, explaining our point of view? That would surely be more reasonable.'

Angie shook her head. 'It wouldn't work—they'd just throw it in the bin. Besides which, if we take them by surprise and picket the place while these films are showing, we'll draw a lot of attention to the problem.'

'I honestly don't think you should encourage the younger nurses to take such action.' The SNO looked doubtful. 'I do sympathise with your feelings, Sister Sinclair, and I think you're right about this kind of thing affecting the way people think of nurses. But I'm not sure that this kind of action is appropriate. I'd be particularly worried if you were to wear your uniforms during something like this. We don't want the hospital brought into ill repute, do we?'

'Ill repute!' Nina and Angie both exploded simultaneously. They exchanged despairing looks across the table. 'Don't you think the hospital authorities should support us in our fight against pornography?'

The SNO looked severe. 'It's not for the hospital to get involved with such issues. If you as individuals wish to take action there's little we can do to stop you, but personally I think you should forget the idea. I'm sure we'd all sign a letter of complaint to the cinema's owners, wouldn't we?' A murmur of solidarity went round the room.

'And are there any other Sisters who would join us in action?' asked Angie. Four hands went up, all of them belonging to the younger staff, and various comments about the offensiveness of the cinema were made. 'Right, then,' said Angie, nodding to Nina and the others, 'I suggest we meet this evening, when we've finished duty, and plan how best to approach this. I don't believe polite letters will do any good at all—and I'm not prepared to put up with walking past the place every day.'

'Four-thirty in the senior staff room?' suggested Nina. There were nods all round.

'I can't say I'm happy with this development,' sighed the SNO, 'but I wish you luck.'

James, still in theatre greens, stood studying the afternoon's operating schedule, looking vainly for a spot in which he could insert an emergency appendectomy who had come in this morning. The white laminated board on which, each day, the theatre administrator scrawled a detailed timetable in felt-tipped pens didn't seem to have a spare inch of room during standard operating hours. He sighed and wrote in his own name, the name of the patient and the number of the theatre he wanted to use on the emergency board, then went off to register his request with Theatres Administration, who would pull together a team of anaesthetist, assistant surgeon, Theatre Sister and nurses so that he could perform the operation after hours.

It would be another late night by the time he'd finished the op, written up his notes and done his post-operative follow-up. That would make his third in a row. And tomorrow he had to be in bright and early to prepare for his Outpatients clinic. For just a few moments he stood looking bleakly at the operating schedule board, not taking in the various coloured squiggles. He was no stranger to hard work, of course, but it was different if you didn't have a proper home to go back to at the end of a long day. A fleeting thought of Abby crept in and caught him unawares, and he had to swallow hard.

He didn't even have any good friends here at the Moorside, not yet. And if he kept working late each evening he wasn't likely to make any either. The urge to fall into a mood of self-pity almost overtook him, but he straightened his shoulders and was about to set off to make arrangements for the appendectomy when Colin Sturgis apprehended him.

'You're coming on Friday night, aren't you?' he asked cheerfully. James grinned curiously.

'Coming where?'

'My stag night party, of course! Don't tell me you haven't been invited?' Colin looked at him in amazement. 'Look, I'm sorry if I didn't get around to it—I've got so much to think about these days! Seriously, I'd like you to come. We haven't had much of a chance to talk and it'll give you an opportunity to meet some of the lads. Most of them are coming, and you're guaranteed a good time.'

'That would be great,' James agreed, feeling his usual enthusiasm creeping back. It always happened; just when he thought he'd reached rock bottom something good turned up. 'I haven't been out much recently, and it's always nice to meet people.'

'Fine.' Colin slapped him heartily on the back. 'We're meeting in the King's Head at six and then we'll find somewhere else to go on to later in the evening. Will that suit you?'

'If I'm not still here,' James laughed, and nodded towards the emergency board where his name was clearly written. 'It seems to be the story of my life these days.'

'Don't worry about it. See you at six at the King's Head,' smiled Colin, backing off down the corridor.

James set off jauntily in the other direction, whistling a cheerful little tune under his breath. A night out with some of the other doctors and surgeons would do him good, give him a chance to get to know them. A night out with a nurse might be better, of course, but then you couldn't have everything. And anyway, he might have chosen the wrong nurse and had a terrible time. He thought of Nina Newington on Men's Surgical. Now there was an example of how a man could get it all wrong. She'd looked so interesting, so attractive . . . and all the while she'd been the most infuriating, irrational person he could ever remember meeting! He felt his teeth clenching in annoyance at the very thought of her, and that annoyed him even more. James had always prided himself on being a calm sort of man. He wasn't easily roused by anyone —and it was a good characteristic to have as a surgeon, where patients could sometimes reduce you to despair or fury. He was easy-going, he knew; there was scarcely anyone he didn't get on with. Except Nina Newington. And as she'd been the one person he'd singled out when he'd arrived, with the idea of getting to know her better, that thought infuriated him. A run-in with a fellow member of the hospital staff he could shake off, that was all in a day's work. But he had rather hoped that he could get to know Sister Newington after work hours, and the knowledge that it was now quite out of the question, and that he had made such a bad judgment about her in the first place, pricked him deeply.

As he was arranging details of the emergency appendectomy down in Theatres, the militant Sisters were collecting a cup of tea in the senior staff sitting room—and among their number was Nina. 'Honestly, it's no wonder that nurses are such a downtrodden lot with those old fuddy-duddys in charge,' grumbled Angie Sinclair as they seated themselves around a low coffee table. 'They look at us as if we're all idiots. They've got to realise that the future of nursing is with us, and that nurses are going to have to change as their jobs change.'

'You've got to admit that you've very outspoken, though,' smiled Nina. 'Not that that's a bad thing, Angie, we all admire the work you've done on the children's ward. But perhaps we ought to take it a bit more slowly in future.'

Angie handed out sheets of paper. 'Unfortunately we don't have any time to waste over this problem. If we don't do it this week, while those films are being shown, our protest will be diluted. The things we've got to aim for are surprise, impact and as much media coverage as possible. Now, where do you think we should start?'

It didn't take long for them to set up the arrangements. Surprisingly, the more they discussed it the more obvious a picket of the cinema seemed to be.

Instead of their enthusiasm waning as they planned it, they all felt more and more strongly that it was the right thing to do. 'Do you think there'll be any trouble?' asked one of the others who was slightly more cautious about it than the rest.

'Trouble? Do you think the owners will call the police?' asked Nina.

'Let them,' smiled one of the others. 'It's a peaceful protest. Anyway, I can't see anyone arresting a nurse for complaining about pornography, can you? With a bit of luck the sympathy will be all on our side.'

Angie ran through her tick list. 'OK, this is what we've agreed to do. I'll type up some notices and stick them all around the hospital. I'll also give out further information to anyone else who's interested. You'll have a chat to staff on other shifts and make sure that they know what's going on,' she said, pointing to one of the other Sisters. 'Carol, you're going to make banners, aren't you? Perhaps we should all make our own too. And Nina, you're going to telephone the local newspapers and the local radio and TV station. You'd better not do that until Friday morning, actually. We don't want word leaking out to the people who own the cinema, so that they can change the films.'

'All right.' Nina wrote it all down. 'And we all meet here, with other nurses who are going to come, at seven on Friday evening?

'That should be all right,' nodded Angie. 'By then there'll be a number of punters inside the cinema and we can embarrass them. And with a bit of luck we'll be able to scare off anyone else who'd intended to go in.'

Nina giggled. 'With us against them, they don't stand a chance!'

'Come in and find yourselves a seat. Bring your coffee with you—I don't suppose there's a chance of another cup for me?' asked Nina, and Kate Hardy zipped back to the kitchen to get one. Nina liked to hold a seminar for her student nurses on Friday afternoons, if there was time. Friday was generally one of their quieter days. Surgeons preferred not to operate on Fridays because they didn't want to have to come in and supervise patients over the weekend, and it was practice to send patients home on a Thursday or a Friday morning if possible. Friday morning often saw a couple of admissions who needed pre-operative investigation or preparation for their op the following week, but they tended not to be cases which required a lot of supervision. Helen and the other staff nurse could cope comfortably during visiting hours, unless there was an emergency admission, in which case the seminar had to be postponed.

Not all Sisters held such informal meetings. They felt that simply showing students how to do certain procedures was enough, and that discussion and theory were best left to Block, as the students' periods of intensive classroom teaching, under the eye of Sister Tutor, was known. But Nina had always found that a chance to talk informally about things that had happened on the ward was invaluable in ensuring that everyone had fully understood how and why the ward was run as it was run. There was a great deal of difference between knowing how a thing was done and *why* it was done, and sometimes, when people's lives were at stake, the why was just as important as the how.

'I thought that today I'd just run over our record-keeping systems with you,' she said, perching casually on the desk. She didn't want to be one of those people who sat firmly on one side of the desk while her students quaked nervously on the other. But oh, how Sister Hallwell would have disapproved, she knew! 'I know that you're probably a bit confused about all the bits of paper that we keep for each patient, so I thought I'd begin by running through them. Do let me know if something doesn't make sense or if you have a question, won't you? That's why we're here.'

The three students nodded in unison. They liked Sister Newington, and not just because she was young like themselves. She was meticulous and hard-working, and she didn't suffer foolishness gladly, but she was also approachable and she didn't make you feel like an idiot if you got something wrong.

'Each patient who is admitted to this ward comes with a set of records, like this.' Nina held up one of the green plastic folders. 'The only exception to this would be an emergency admission who wasn't known to this hospital. But most people are referred here by their GPs and they have a full set of medical records, including Outpatients reports and

GPs' reports. When they're admitted to the ward the medical department sends their records here with them, and they're kept on file here for reference.' She pointed to the top drawer of her filing cabinet. 'They're kept in a locked drawer because they're confidential, as you know. Now, when the patient comes in it's very important to check that we have the right notes for him.'

Jane giggled. 'I suppose that's so that you don't perform the wrong operation on him.'

'It *has* happened, I assure you. For example, you've only been on this ward for ten days. Yet how many patients called Williams have we had in that time?' The students turned to each other. Two? Three?

'We've actually had four Williamses—you're forgetting that overnight emergency who was transferred to Stoke Mandeville. Now it could have been easy to muddle up those people, so when they're admitted you don't just take it for granted that you have the right person. You gently question them about their initials and addresses, and if necessary about their medical condition, and check the information against their files. Then, when you're sure that you have the right person, you take all the relevant information about their current condition and the notes about their surgeon or consultant, and you fill out a Kardex record sheet for them. The sheet is then inserted into the loose-leaf file in alphabetical order.' Nina flicked through a couple of sheets. 'You're all, I hope, familiar with this system?' There were nods all round. 'Kate, just run through, if you will, the information that can be recorded on this sheet.'

'Basic things like name and ward and the date of admission. Details about the patient's surgical and medical history, if necessary . . .'

'Some surgeons and consultants actually like to go through the patient's records and decide for themselves what they want to include on the Kardex,' Nina butted in. 'Others leave it to the nursing staff. What would you keep a special look-for if you were filling in the records?'

'Previous conditions which might affect the current problem,' offered Kate.

'Allergies, adverse previous reactions to drugs,' suggested Ginette.

'How about personal details that might be relevant—like an elderly person who has no one at home to look after them?' asked Jane.

'Yes, all of this could be relevant and should be immediately accessible,' agreed Nina. 'I suggest that when you have a few spare moments you take a look through here and note the kind of details that are important. I interrupted Kate just now, so I'll finish off her answer for her. As well as all these details the Kardex file contains a complete treatment record for each patient. Each time a doctor orders a treatment, or a change in the treatment, or ceases a treatment, we record it in here. Before the days of the Kardex nurses had to spend hours each day copying details of treatments into a daily treatment book. Now it all goes straight into the Kardex. Every dose and every injection is recorded here. It means that we can have a complete record on just the one sheet. I know that you think it's a bore to have to constantly consult it and fill it in, but I assure you that it really makes life easier.'

'Does the doctor just tell you that he wants a treatment changing?' asked Ginette. The other two students looked up at the ceiling in mock-disgust. Of the three Ginette was the slowest. She was a placid, kind girl, inclined to daydream, and Nina was never sure how much she had actually taken in or whether that slight smile and calm gaze indicated that she had no idea what was happening.

'The doctor or surgeon in charge of each case keeps a separate prescription sheet for each patient. They're kept here. I transfer the details to the Kardex, to keep the records up to date. For regular medication—every four hours, for example—the prescription sheet goes round with the medicine trolley. You consult each patient's sheet before administering the drugs, and you fill in the time and drug and initial the drugs book every time a dose is given. For one-off or irregular treatments I draw up and supervise a special daily chart, like this.' Nina showed them the day's chart. 'Can you see that we started off with a pre-med for Mr Hungerford at eight-thirty? Then Mr Clark was ordered to have morphine as required and I've made a note here for a three-hourly top-up. Because we have to make individual arrangements, we have constantly to be checking times, doses and special requirements.'

'It gets quite complicated, doesn't it? Do you ever miss a dose, Sister?' asked Kate cheekily.

'It's almost inevitable that from time to time, particularly if there's an emergency admission, a patient on a special course of treatment will receive a dose a bit later or earlier than planned,' Nina admitted. 'If you get yourself into a situation where for some reason a patient misses a dose altogether —and it *has* been known to happen—it's best to come clean and contact the doctor in charge. Don't go forging the drugs book by filling in your initials and the correct time. A missed dose in a course of treatment may have considerable effects on the efficacy of the treatment. It may endanger the whole course. So let the doctor know. Naturally he won't be pleased, but he'll prefer to know about it rather than to be left in the dark. Of course, most patients will tell you if you're late with their medicine, particularly those who are reasonably well and with nothing to do but watch the clock . . .'

'Like Mr Wells. You only have to be two minutes late with anything and he makes a terrible fuss!'

'In future,' smiled Nina, 'be grateful to him. There are other things I want to discuss with you, like the importance of our three-line charts, which you help to keep when you do your four-hourly checks. I also want to run through the routines for sending and receiving samples for the path. lab. But for now I think we'll finish on a word of warning regarding X-rays.'

From the desk she picked up a blotchy, opaque X-ray film. 'This is what happens when you get an X-ray wet—it's ruined. This accident occurred this morning, when Mr Farris put it down on a wet locker top. There are two lessons to be learnt from this. The first is, don't ever put an X-ray down on anything damp. And the second is that even if a surgeon does so he'll always find a way of blaming you for allowing the locker top to get damp in the first place.'

'You can't win, can you?' sighed Jane.

'Some people would be reasonable about it. Others, as you say, Jane, will always find someone to shift the blame on to.' Nina was tight-lipped. How was she to have known that a patient had tipped a vase of flowers over and hadn't called a nurse to have the mess mopped up properly? Anyway, James Farris should have given *her* the film to hold, not just slapped it down in the first spot that he saw. And then he'd gone and topped off the whole thing with some caustic remark, asking her if she was trying to sabotage the treatment of his patient. Naturally he had been put out; the X-ray was the only one which showed the patient's colon at full extension—but there was no need to be so churlish about it. And what irked even more was the fact that he was so well liked by everyone. The nurses thought he was terrific, judging from the various remarks that she had overheard in the canteen and in passing. Even Angie Sinclair, who had met him at the same party as Nina, had said how good-looking and friendly he was. Nina felt left out. James Farris was deliberately going out of his way to be nice to everyone except her, and with her he was as scathing as he could be. She wondered fleetingly what was wrong with her. Why did he treat her so differently from everyone else? In her heart, of course, she knew. She had been offhand with him from the start and he had obviously vowed to treat her in the same manner. Well, despite the fact that she wouldn't mind being on the receiving end of one of his smiles, she wasn't going to be the first to give in. No, he was a chauvinist pig, he'd made that perfectly clear, and she was not going to make any reconciliatory gestures.

'That's it for this afternoon,' she said briskly, emerging from her private thoughts with a start. The students were looking at her curiously and she wondered with some confusion whether she had actually spoken them aloud. 'It's tea time and you'll be needed on the ward.'

'Oh, Sister,' said Kate as she stacked her chair back against the wall, 'we'll be coming to the picket this evening at the cinema, if that's all right.'

'Of course it's all right,' smiled Nina. 'I'll see you there, then. But now I've got to get on with all my paperwork.' The students left the office and she turned to confront the desk, still loaded with forms and reports and records. Paperwork, paperwork —would there ever be an end to it?

CHAPTER THREE

'HERE you are!' Angie Sinclair, surrounded by at least a dozen nurses, stood in front of a seedy little cinema in the main road just a few hundred yards from the Moorside. 'I thought you'd lost your nerve. Which banner do you want? I've only got three left.'

Nina looked at the three cardboard placards Angie was offering. 'It's a good turnout, isn't it?' she commented. Jane, Kate and four other students had just arrived with her and there were more on the way. It looked as if there might be thirty or more nurses there, all in their uniforms, to protest. 'I think I'll take NURSES ARE LIFE-SAVERS, NOT SEX SYMBOLS,' she said, turning down the other two placards, which were immediately grabbed by other nurses. NURSES CAN'T AFFORD BLACK STOCKINGS, read one, and NURSES' SECRETS—LOW PAY & LONG HOURS read the other. 'Now what do we do?'

'Did you phone the local paper and tell them what was happening?' asked Angie.

'Yes, they said they'd be here. And I called the radio and television stations too. Both said they'd be interested. Oh, look, here comes someone now!' A young man carrying a large black box slung over his shoulders approached them.

53

'Is Nina Newington here?' he asked, glancing at all the nurses who had formed a grey and lilac barricade around the front of the cinema. A small crowd of onlookers had already gathered and some of the student nurses were handing out photo-copied leaflets explaining the reasons that they were blocking the pavement.

'Yes, I'm Nina.' Suddenly she felt nervous. They had organised this thing so quickly, without much thought for the consequences, that it seemed like a game.

'My name's Dick Marsh, I'm from the local radio. I wondered whether you'd like to say a few words—explain what you're doing here and why.' Nina swallowed a lump in her throat and nodded. Out of the corner of her eye she could see a photographer, obviously a professional, judging by the size of his camera, taking pictures. Angie had slipped away from her side and was talking to a man with a large notebook, who was jotting down her words. 'Just speak into this—give me your name, the ward you work on and your position,' said the man with the tape recorder, which was now revealed as he flipped back the black leather and a dozen shining knobs and buttons came into view. 'If you could waffle on for a second it would help me adjust the sound balance,' he added encouragingly.

'I'm Nina Newington . . .' He jammed the microphone firmly under her nose, 'and I'm Acting Sister on the Men's Surgical ward at Moorside Hospital, which is just up the road.'

With an encouraging thumbs-up sign he withdrew the microphone, spoke into it, 'Perhaps you'd like to tell me why you and fifty other nurses from the hospital are demonstrating here, outside the Regal Cinema this evening,' and he shoved it back into her face.

Quite how she managed it, Nina never knew. There was some shouting in the background as staff from the cinema emerged and tried to make the nurses go away, and the hubbub from the gathering crowd grew in volume. Nevertheless she managed to concentrate on the interviewer's questions and speak without too many umms and ers, telling him about the problems faced by nurses these days, the increasing harassment and the objections of Moorside staff to having a sex cinema just down the road. 'Terrific,' said Dick Marsh as he wound it up with a professional flourish. 'I've got to go and speak to the cinema manager now. See you later—and don't worry, everyone's on your side.'

When she turned back to the crowds, Nina was aghast at the number who had congregated, completely blocking the path at the side of the cinema and spilling into the road. Angie was now standing in front of one of the displays showing scantily-clad nurses clambering all over men who, because of their stethoscopes, one had to presume were doctors—they seemed to be wearing nothing else—and talking animatedly into the video camera wielded by a crew from the regional TV station. Kate and Jane and half a dozen other students were telling a news reporter how much they earned a month as well as their objections to the Regal's latest films. And standing along the pavements, shouting encouragement, was a motley crowd of old ladies, small boys and women with shopping.

'Angels, that's what these nurses are,' a decrepit old gentleman was telling the camera as he gave Angie a grateful kiss. 'Had my prostate done the year before last, and they looked after me champion. They deserve better than this . . .' It was obvious that the media loved it—pretty young nurses, surviving on a pittance and saving the lives of the sick and vulnerable.

'Do you think this kind of film makes men go out and rape women?' asked another reporter, pencil poised to take down every word that Nina could come out with.

'Well, I wouldn't go so far as to . . . Psychologists can't actually prove that there's a direct link between . . .' she vacillated. But the reporter's interest had lapsed, because a new cry had gone up.

'They're coming out!'

A trickle of men, quite unsuspecting what was going on outside, had emerged from the cinema's doors. Squinting because of the sudden light after almost an hour in the dark, they found themselves suddenly surrounded by banner-waving nurses. 'You should be ashamed of yourself!' a nurse yelled, and there was immediately a chorus of catcalls. 'Does your wife know you're here?' 'Would you like to take on this naughty nurse, buster?' Sheepishly the men made their way through the crowd, heads down—and as they passed by a new sound rose.

'Oh, my goodness, it's Mr Sturgis!' Kate's stunned tones made Nina look more closely. 'And Mr Nash and Mr Wainwright from Radiology. And look, there's Mr Farris!'

'These are doctors from the hospital?' the reporter at her elbow asked incredulously. Nina nodded, so furious that she couldn't speak. 'This will make a brilliant story,' said the newspaper man. 'Excuse me!' he reached out and caught the sleeve of James Farris, who struggled to follow his friends but was soon surrounded by aghast nurses.

'Look, we don't make a habit of this,' James tried to explain. 'Colin Sturgis is getting married tomorrow and we thought we'd all go out to celebrate, that's all.'

His explanation was to everyone, not just to the reporter, who still had hold of him and was plying him with questions. 'It wasn't my idea to come!' He was already bright pink and shrinking with embarrassment, and he went even redder now, as he set eyes on Nina, standing just a few feet away but so blazing with fury that he could feel the heat already. 'I have no comment to make,' he finished, but the reporter still kept throwing questions at him. Didn't he think it was somewhat irresponsible for doctors to see such films when they'd spent all day working with nurses? Didn't he understand why the nurses were so upset?

'It's all just a joke, a terrible misunderstanding,' said Colin Sturgis, fighting his way back through the crowd to rescue James, who was looking so embarrassed that he might have curled up and died at any moment.

The reporter turned his attention from James to Colin Sturgis, and James tried to take a few steps through the seething mass of nurses—until he was stopped short by Nina. 'This is awful!' He tried to smile ruefully, but it didn't work. Inside he felt like crying. He hadn't wanted to come here in the first place. Dirty films had never been his cup of tea, they embarrassed and offended him. He didn't see how anyone who treated people's bodies, particularly women's bodies, could justify looking at them. He'd protested, tried to get the others to go for a meal or a few more drinks, but Colin had insisted that on his last night of freedom he wanted to see something blue. Not that the films had been as salacious as the carefully calculated publicity had led them to expect.

Now, with a sickening thud, he knew what a terrible mistake he'd made. 'Sister Newington—I'm sorry,' he muttered, standing there abjectly. 'Sister Sinclair . . . Nurse Bond . . .' Appalled, he looked around and registered the faces that he knew. 'I don't normally come here. I've never been to anything like this before in my life!' he tried to explain.

'Is that supposed to make it any better?' snapped Nina. 'Mr Farris, from the moment I met you I knew you were the worst chauvinist I'd ever met. You refused to remove a patient who was making a nuisance of himself from my ward and you called my opinions loony feminist nonsense. And now look at you! And you expect us to work with you again! You're disgusting!'

'Yes,' piped up a student nurse at her side, 'we all know what you've been ogling!'

'Please, it's not like that!' James looked around him helplessly. Colin Sturgis had been cornered by the video team and was having an animated argument with Angie Sinclair, and two of the other doctors were standing talking uncomfortably to the man with the tape recorder. 'Honestly, I'm very embarrassed and deeply regret——'

'Deeply regret! That's not a lot of use when we have to co-operate with you, is it?'

'For God's sake, Nina,' James appealed, using her christian name without thinking, because despite everything that had happened between them, he still thought of her as Nina and not Sister Newington, 'don't make things any worse. Just let me through. Please!'

'No way. You need a lesson, Mr Farris.' She was surprised at his appeal, surprised that he had used her name. For a second she felt like saying, 'All right, I'll let you off this once,' as if she was talking to a little boy. But she didn't. She stood squarely and held up the banner so that he could read it.

James tried to push his way through. If he could get away now he might escape the attention of the local media. 'That's enough of this nonsense——'

He was stopped in his stride as Nina brought her banner down firmly on the back of his neck. It was only made of cardboard and plywood, but it was enough to surprise him and make him trip over. He crashed down among them. It is a nurse's reflex action to go to the aid of anyone in distress, and in a split second, immediately regretting what she had done, Nina was down on the pavement beside him.

'Are you all right?' The question sounded more desperate than she had intended it to. The words 'I'm sorry' hovered on her tongue, but she didn't have a chance to get them out.

'You'll have to hit me a damn sight harder than that if you want to finish me off, Sister Newington.' James got to his feet as elegantly as he could and brushed down his dark cream trousers which had a tell-tale black smudge at the knee. He glowered down at her, and for the first time she realised how big he was—not just tall, though he was at least six feet, but also broad-shouldered with it. If he'd hit her now, and she couldn't help but feeling that he had every right to, she wouldn't have a chance. 'You're crazy, did you know that? You can get away with all sorts of things by classing them under the title of women's oppression. You can call me all the names you like, hit me, ruin my reputation in public, and all in the name of Women's Liberation!'

'How dare you?' cried Nina. 'Just like a man, turning it all back on us. I suppose it's *my* fault that you came to see this dirty little peep-show today?'

'It's women like you that make men into sexists,' James retorted. 'I'm getting out of here, and you're not going to stop me.'

'Grrr!' All thoughts of apology fled from her now. 'I am!' Without thought for what she was doing, Nina batted him round the head again with the placard. He grabbed it from her and broke it efficiently into two over his knee—and at that moment the policeman arrived.

'You all right, sir?' he enquired. Nina suddenly realised how quiet everyone had gone. The laughter and the shouts had died now.

'That's a fine thing, isn't it?' she snapped hotheadedly. 'Do you really think I could do him any damage?'

'Not really, miss—but I did see you hit him,' the policeman said sternly, 'and it might look better if you allow him to speak for himself.'

'Thank you, officer.' James gave her a withering look. 'I'm quite all right. I just wanted to get away from here, that was all—and I experienced some difficulty.' He shot Nina another meaningful glance.

'Now you know you shouldn't be obstructing people,' warned the man in blue, who also towered above her. 'I suggest you go home, miss, and let yourself calm down.'

'Calm down!' Nina was indignant. She knew she shouldn't lose her temper, particularly not with a policeman, but she couldn't help herself. 'Do you know who this man is?'

'No, I don't, miss,' said the policeman patiently. 'And as far as I can see he's done nothing wrong.'

'This man,' Nina pointed accusingly, her black brows drawing into a tight line, 'is a surgeon at Moorside Hospital.'

'I've no doubt he is.' James and the policeman looked at her and she thought she saw a kind of smugness on their faces, as if the two of them were deliberately ganging up against her. Just like two men in positions of authority to support each other when right was clearly on her side.

'This is appalling! These men have spent the evening watching pornographic films while we've staged a peaceful picket, and now you're just going to let them go free! It's a male conspiracy; when it comes to the crunch you all stick together!' She could hear her own voice, and she knew she was going over the top, but somehow, for some reason, she couldn't stop herself. And the sight of James Farris standing there glowering with his hands in his pockets made it all ten times worse. She wouldn't have been so wild if it had been any other surgeon in the hospital. He got to her in a way that no other member of staff did. 'It's all your fault!' she spat.

'OK, I think we've had quite enough, thank you.' The policeman took her firmly by the shoulder. 'I think perhaps you'd better come with me.'

James stepped forward. 'There's really no need —honestly, officer, there's no point in taking any notice of her. She'll cool down in a minute, when she realises that this has all gone too far.'

'She can come and cool down in the police station,' said the policeman, and before she could overcome her shock Nina found herself being led through the crowd, who had now begun to boo, and bundled into the back seat of a police car. The last thing she saw, as the car pulled out into the traffic, where now police reinforcements had arrived to

break up the demonstration, was James's startled
face gazing blankly after her.

The policewoman who looked after her at the
station was actually very kind. 'You nurses must
have a lot to put up with,' she said sympathetically,
when Nina had explained what had happened. 'We
all know what a tough job it is, dealing with the
public—and at least we're better paid than you
are.' Then she'd brought her a cup of tea and a
biscuit.

'Do you think I'm going to be charged?' Nina
asked quietly. Why, oh, why couldn't she control
her temper? She looked bleakly round the pale
green walls of the interview room and felt tears
rising to her eyes. It was always like this. She got
angry, said things that she fervently believed at the
time, and then found herself in hot water for it.

'No, I shouldn't think so,' said the policewoman
reassuringly. 'You really were just brought in to
calm down. Drink your tea and then we'll see what
we can do.'

But Nina didn't even have time to finish the cup
before the policeman who had arrested her entered
the room. 'I hadn't realised that it was a domestic
tiff out there in front of the cinema,' he said with a
sly smile. 'Your boyfriend's just come in and explained everything.'

'My boyfriend?' Nina peered at him over the rim
of the cup.

'That's right. He's explained why you were so
furious with him for going to see that film.' He
chuckled under his breath. 'In the circumstances I

can imagine my wife hitting me over the head too!'

'I don't think I . . .' Nina faltered.

'Don't worry.' The policeman got to his feet. 'We'll say no more about it, eh? Just don't have your tiffs in public in future, or you could find yourself in real trouble next time.' He gestured out through the door. 'He's here, waiting for you.'

Nina got reluctantly to her feet. She didn't understand what was happening, but it seemed that she was free to go, though they'd obviously got her muddled up with someone else. She picked up her coat and bag and said thank you to both police officers. Then she walked from the interview room and down the short corridor to the reception desk. A familiar figure, six foot tall and with sandy hair, greeted her. 'Hallo, Nina—*darling*,' he added for good measure, making faces at her to indicate that she should reciprocate.

'What are *you* doing here?' she asked coldly.

James's face lost some of its friendliness. 'I came to bail you out,' he said jokingly to the policeman behind the desk. 'I explained that you were entitled to take a swipe at me because we lived together.'

'You *what*?' Nina's look could have frozen a puddle at ten paces.

'There's gratitude!' James shrugged his shoulders with mock despair and the policeman laughed. 'Come on, let's go.' He held out his hand to her. She didn't move.

'And where are we going?' she demanded, her head slightly to one side. He'd started them on this caper, so let him go on with it.

'Nineteen, Arcadia Gardens.' The address made her start with shock. 'Where we both live.' He said it with such firmness that she felt herself propelled towards him. She was going to live at nineteen, Arcadia Gardens. She'd told the estate agent and the solicitor and the building society that she was buying the top floor flat there. For a minute she thought she was going to be sick, there and then, on the police station's polished lino floor. Then James's strong arm was around her. 'Come on, love, let's go home.' And they were out into the fresh air, with the policeman behind the desk laughing quietly to himself. Women! Who would ever understand them?

'You own the house in Arcadia Gardens?' James nodded and went on tucking into his bacon, lettuce and tomato sandwich. 'And I'm going to be living upstairs from you?' He nodded again. 'And you just told those policemen that we were living together and I hit you and got so furious because I'd just caught you coming out of that cinema?' Another nod. 'You've got a bloody nerve, Mr Farris!' Nina's words weren't much more than a whisper. She didn't want another row, not here in the bistro into which he had dragged her.

He looked quizzically at her. 'Really? I thought it was quite noble of me, bearing in mind all the things you've said and done to me recently. And do you really mean that you had no idea that I owned the house?'

'None at all!' Nina shot back. 'If I'd known

you owned it I'd never have got past the front door!'

'Don't be so childish,' he said calmly, taking another mouthful. There was a silence while Nina let it all sink in. And maybe, perhaps maybe, she *had* reacted a little drastically.

'When did *you* find out I was the buyer?' she asked at last.

'This afternoon, when I went to my solicitor to check up on the contracts. And there was your name and address right at the top of the file.' James looked at her and smiled. 'Just think—we're going to be neighbours!'

'Not if I can help it,' she muttered, taking a nibble from her cannelloni. 'It's still not too late to cancel the whole thing.'

James shrugged. When she was like this, rueful and quiet, he liked her. When she was furious, yelling at him and being so silly, he still rather liked her. She made him want to gather her up in his arms and hug her and make her stop being stupid. It was irrational, he knew, because she obviously had a profound dislike of him. It hurt him. 'You'll lose money,' he said matter-of-factly. 'Your solicitor, the survey, my solicitor's fees . . .'

'I'm not paying for *your* solicitor!'

'You might have to if you pull out for no reason,' he pointed out. Nina squirmed in her seat.

'We're not going to be very good neighbours,' she said suddenly.

'Speak for yourself,' James said affably. It was his almost constant cheerfulness that irked Nina more than anything. If he'd been angry or nasty she could feel justified in being rude to him, but he was so darned pleasant about the whole thing. It was as much as she could do not to smile at him.

'I'm a very good neighbour—always ready to help out with lightbulbs and plugs and the odd bit of do-it-yourself.'

'I won't need that kind of help, thank you,' Nina said ungraciously. 'I've got friends to help with that kind of thing—though I can do most of it myself.'

James tried to look nonchalant, but the thought that she probably had a boyfriend somewhere recurred to him. Someone as outgoing and vivacious as this girl would surely have a man—or men—in tow. She was very attractive in a dark, firecracker kind of way. He admired her neat profile even as she frowned disapprovingly at him. 'What do you think will happen after tonight's adventure?' she asked quickly. For a minute her aggression seemed to falter. 'Do you think I'll get fired?'

He shrugged, but she noticed that his forehead furrowed too. He was not as unconcerned about it as he seemed. 'Neither of us did anything illegal and the police didn't charge you. I'll probably get dragged over the coals by the Head of Surgery if anyone gets to hear of it. You nurses were in the right, so even if you get a ticking off I don't suppose you'll have anything to fear about your jobs——'

'So you admit that you were in the wrong going into that cinema in the first place?'

James looked pained. 'Of course I do! I apologised right there and then on the spot, if you remember. You were probably in too much of a state,' he added darkly, 'to hear a word I said.'

Nina grimaced. 'I seem to remember that you were wittering on about not wanting to go in there in the first place.' She shot him a reproving glance. 'Honestly, I don't know what I'm doing here having dinner with you.'

'Think of me as your white knight without a charger—I *did* come and rescue you from the cells, remember.' He smiled.

'How patronising! You don't really believe that women still believe in things like that, do you? The Sisters are doing it for themselves these days, Mr Farris,' she snapped.

'And getting into trouble too,' he observed wryly. 'You may not believe in it, but I do. I still believe that somewhere out there there's someone special. And please call me James, not Mr Farris. I feel about sixty when you do that!'

Nina reached for her purse and found the right money for her half of the bill. 'Well, James, I've got to go.' She stood up and collected her bag. 'I feel an idiot sitting in here in my uniform anyway.'

'I'll pick up the tab for both of us.' James tried to hand her back the money. 'Come on, I earn twice as much as you and you need all the cash you can get at the moment. Buying a place is expensive.'

Nina turned to face him. Her lips were set and her eyebrows were just beginning to dip menacingly. 'Haven't you heard a word I've said? Maybe there are some women who want to be looked after like a china doll, rescued by knights on white chargers, have their bills paid for them, all that kind of thing—but I'm not one of them, you know. I don't need your patronage.'

James pocketed her money, his head down so that she couldn't see what was going on in those blue eyes. When he finally looked up she sensed that she'd pricked him deeply in some way. 'I'm trying to be friendly, Nina, that's all there is to it. You need the money, I don't. There's nothing patronising about it. I'm not trying to buy you in some way.' He swallowed. 'Someone, at some time, must have been really nasty to you to make you like this. You don't seem to be able to take anything in the spirit in which it's offered.' And with that he put his wallet in his pocket and walked out of the restaurant.

Heads turned. After all, it wasn't usual to see a man walk out and leave a woman just standing there. Feeling suddenly uncomfortable, Nina called over the waitress and paid the bill. The girl looked at her curiously, eyebrows raised. 'Men!' said Nina simply, pulling an agonised face.

The waitress nodded agreement. 'Men!'

CHAPTER FOUR

IT WAS a twenty-minute walk back to the flat that Nina shared with one of her old friends, Anna, who was an articled clerk. They had known each other at school, lost touch and then, by a stroke of coincidence, met up with each other a year or two ago at a time when they had both been looking for a flatshare. Nina was pleased not to be sharing with another nurse. She had had enough of that during her training and early years at the hospital. It was good to come home to someone who hadn't been near the hospital all day and had stories of their own to tell. But now Anna was moving to London where she could complete her solicitor's training —and that was the reason why Nina was buying her own place.

When she got back to the flat it was empty. Anna was obviously out for the evening. Nina stripped out of her uniform and had a shower, but for some reason she couldn't stop brooding. Whether it was because, deep down, she was nervous of what would happen tomorrow at the hospital she didn't know. And some of it, she reasoned, had to be delayed shock from being taken away by the police. But there was something else too. James Farris's words kept echoing in her mind. 'Someone must have been really nasty to you to make you like this . . .', that was what he'd said. How could he possibly know? No one at the hospital knew anything about it, so he couldn't have heard on the grapevine. It bothered her. What had happened in the past was entirely her own affair, nothing to do with him. She felt annoyance beginning to rise in her at the thought of him. Oh, he was a meddling, interfering busybody! Why did he have to be so polite and gentlemanly? He was about the least arrogant surgeon in the entire hospital, so why did he make her feel so angry?

Nina went and dug her memento box out from under the bed in her room. The place was decorated in strong colours, the kind of colours she felt happy in. No wishy-washy pinks or beiges. The Duvet was covered in crisp emerald green and white striped fabric and one wall had matching green and white trellis-effect wallpaper. There was a squashy armchair in scarlet quilting and a bright red reading lamp. She sat on the bed and opened her photograph album. Whenever the past began to hurt her she always did this, confronting it rather than trying to hide from it. 1983. 1984. She stopped, then turned the pages more slowly. Many of the faces were the same close friends and family. Then a new one appeared—a face which thereafter appeared in almost every picture. Nina left the album open at one which showed her sitting on the old swing that hung from an apple tree at home. There she was, happy in her jeans and sweatshirt —and there was Alan, smiling and looking for all the world as if he was having a good time. Of course, he couldn't have been, because only a few hours later he'd told her that it was all over. Nina ran her finger over her own smiling face and wondered what it would have been like if he hadn't told her what he did . . .

She had met Alan Gill when she was out on secondment for her midwifery top-up course. The facilities at Moorside were limited, so she had gone for six weeks, with just one other girl, to work and study in the Obstetrics department of the county hospital in York. Alan Gill had been an anaesthetist there, devastatingly good-looking and full of fun. Nina had met him during her first week and within three days had been hopelessly in love. What was more, it had been reciprocated—or so she'd thought. He had become her lover, and she had almost lived with him in his hospital flat. It had all happened so fast, quite unlike what she had imagined love would be.

She'd thought that, being such a sensible person, it would come slowly. Instead, within a month they were talking about marrying. Alan had even investigated the possibility of buying a house somewhere between York and Moorside, so that they could both continue their work. Her parents had liked him too—until, of course, the day that he had come to visit her at home and confessed something that had taken her weeks to actually believe was true. He was married. His wife was a research scientist who had moved down to Cambridge; he had only three more weeks to serve at the hospital before he followed her to Addenbrookes. He'd already bought a house—in Cambridge. He was only living in a hospital flat in York because he had already sold their home. And althought he kept saying that he *did* love her, he had no intention of leaving his wife to be with Nina.

At the time she had thought that she would never get over it. She had never trusted a man before, not to that extent. She had been so sure that Alan was the one for her, never a doubt in her head. She wasn't stupid; she wasn't one of those girls who constantly falls in and out of love with every attractive man who came along. She had told herself time and time again that Alan was too good to be true—but he had always proved himself true, until that last day.

Now, with the benefit of hindsight and a couple more years' experience of life, Nina could see that Alan had in fact been a weak kind of man. He had had a certain superficial kind of glamour, the kind that came automatically with good looks and a winning personality. But he had taken the easy way out. After meeting her and bowling her over he had never had the strength of character to come clean about his marriage. In fact he really *had* allowed himself to fall in love with her. It was as if he had completely wiped out his wife and all his other responsibilities. Perhaps they'd frightened him; perhaps he didn't want to move to Cambridge, so he had pretended to her and to himself that he wasn't going. He hadn't meant to deceive and hurt her, she accepted that. But it was because he was weak and unwilling to break the affair off at an early stage that he had succeeded in wounding her so deeply. No one at Moorside had got to hear about it, thank goodness. The other nurse, the one who had been seconded with her, had caught chicken pox from a child in Paediatrics soon after arriving and had not the slightest inkling that Nina was spicing her study of obstetrics with a passionate affair with a married man.

After that she had come back to Moorside, and just a week or two later met Anna who, though not aware of the full details, had an intuitive idea of what had happened. Together they had found this flat and together they had gone along to some meetings of a local women's group. Anna was a firm feminist—she said that working in the law you had to be, or you got trampled on by dozens of eager male graduates—and Nina had begun to change her ideas too. Not that she believed that men were the enemy, as so many of the girls she had met there did. But it helped to open her eyes to some of the goings-on in the hospital; and it helped her to cope with what Alan had done.

In a way, getting involved with Alan Gill had been the best thing that had ever happened to her, she thought perversely. Because of him she had learned to think more deeply about herself, and the business of nursing, and the way the hospital and the world was run. True, she had to put up with the reputation of being one of Moorside's feminist Sisters, like Angie Sinclair. Some of the most narrow-minded and piggish doctors got a lot of pleasure out of taunting them for it. But she had also got respect from some of the other staff, like Sister Parker who had selected her for training for Sister because, she said, Nina had a mind of her own. Why were she and Angie so eccentric, just because they had raised the problem of how some of the hospital's gynaecologists, all of them men, manipulated and forced the women in their care to do things they didn't want them to do? Why did some obstetricians take a perverse pleasure in insisting that women in labour should lie flat on their backs when they were desperate to get up and walk around, or crouch on all fours? Why had doctors encroached on the traditionally female role of the midwife, to the extent that the midwife's job had all but disappeared in some parts of the country?

With Angie and a couple of other nurses from the hospital Nina had attended special seminars and lectures on these problems within medicine. They had actually taken the time and trouble to think and care about what was going on. They had pondered the subject deeply, while the people who jokingly called them militants hadn't given the subject a moment's thought. That was what made Nina so angry. Hospitals were like a small version of the world at large. They were full of talented, capable women who were being held back—not just by men but by other women, like some of those older Sisters, who believed despite the evidence of their ears and eyes over the years that doctors and surgeons were a race apart—a race to whom the nurses dared not aspire. Know your place—you're only a nurse, they seemed to warn each time she or

Angie or one of the other Sisters pushed for change. That was why nurses like Sister Parker were leaving the hospital and going into administration. As nurses they knew they could do more, take more responsibility and provide more care, but they weren't allowed to.

The front door slammed. Nina put away her memento box. She didn't want Anna to find her mooning over it and the old times. She'd put all that behind her, and she was better for it. Nina thought again of James Farris's parting remark. Perhaps she had been very sharp with him, but it was nothing more than he deserved. He was a bit different from the other doctors he seemed to hang around with. She actually believed him when he said that he hadn't wanted to go to that film at the Regal. But she would have admired him a bit more if he'd had the backbone to refuse. That was the problem with men. They had a herd instinct, like sheep. If one went, they all went. It was what they were taught on the playing fields of the world's public schools. Despite that, she didn't feel unduly proud of the way she had treated him. If men were patronising idiots, like Colin Sturgis, the urological surgeon, it didn't matter what they thought of you. James Farris obviously had a little more between the ears than most—and he was more genuine than most too.

She got up and paced the room, drawing the curtains. Already, in preparation for moving, she had begun to pack her books and records into a couple of strong cardboard boxes. With a bit of luck it would only be a matter of three or four weeks before she could move into her very own place. Again she thought of James Farris. Her threat to call the whole move off had been a bluff. It had taken her months to find a place she liked at a price she could afford and she wasn't going to let it go now, not even if the world's worst chauvinist pig was going to be her neighbour. What had he said this evening? 'Someone must have been really nasty to you to make you like this . . .' If by 'this' he meant strong-willed and independent, she didn't mind. Just because he obviously preferred his women to be like compliant marshmallows! Yet there had been a touch of pity somewhere in that remark, as if he felt sorry for her. Now that really *did* infuriate her. Who was he to take pity on her? She didn't need it and she didn't want it. Just because he wanted to patronise her and treat her like some poor creature worth his sympathy—that was *his* problem. She kicked the red chair hard, forgetting she had no shoes on, and the pain of her stubbed toes quite drove any thought of men, and James Farris in particular, out of her head.

Sundays were, in many ways, the best day of the week on the ward. There were no consultants' rounds, none of the routine visits from doctors or blood-takers, no ward clerk bustling about or porters in and out with trolleys. Nina enjoyed working on Sunday, which was a good job really, as she had to work one in four of them. Because it was quieter she could work with the students, demonstrating and overseeing them as they learned the kind of skills they would need throughout their nursing careers.

'Right, Kate,' she called this morning. 'Let's take Mr Nicholson's stitches out, shall we?' Kate, who had been dawdling round the ward checking that everyone who wanted one had a Sunday paper, practically skipped down to the dressings room. 'What are we going to need?' asked Nina. She showed Kate Mr Nicholson's notes.

'A standard dressings tray,' murmured Kate, reading the surgeon's details. 'I see that the wound was closed with skin clips, so we'll need the special removal forceps.'

'Right, lay the tray up.' Nina stood and watched as Kate went capably about her business, scrubbing up and laying out the sterile instruments with care. Nina felt pleased with her. She was a bright girl, and willing too. She actually seemed to enjoy the challenge of doing something new—unlike Ginette, who seemed to want to hide whenever she was asked to do something for the first time.

'Sister?' Kate asked, laying the gauze dressings in their packs by the side of the bowl with its dressings forceps.

'Mm?' Nina added a pack of Melolin, just in case it was needed.

'Did everything turn out all right on Friday night?' Kate looked at her nervously. 'Mr Farris said he'd go straight to the police station and explain. We would have come, but Sister Sinclair told us it was better for everyone to go home. She nearly got arrested too.'

'I know. I had lunch with her yesterday and we've had the post-mortem. Did you see the papers yesterday?'

Kate grimaced. 'Yes. After all that effort, and we're upstaged!'

Nina couldn't help thinking to herself that perhaps it was for the best that there had been a huge warehouse fire only an hour or two after the picket of the cinema had ended. The front page of yesterday's local paper had been devoted to it and the nurses' demonstration had been demoted to two columns and a rather out-of-focus picture of Angie holding her placard. There were brief mentions of 'heated exchanges' and a note that some of the customers of the cinema were local doctors on a stag night out, but the guilty parties weren't named, to Nina's disgust. Nor, to her relief, was she. The fact that she had been taken away by the police seemed to quite have escaped everyone's notice. It was a damp squib—but she couldn't help being pleased that it was.

Kate had finished and stood surveying her handiwork. 'But Mr Farris did go to the police station, did he? We were all very worried about you. You needed rescuing.'

'I did not need rescuing, as you put it,' Nina retorted. 'Mr Farris turned up too late to be any use at all. I was just about to go when he strolled in and made a nuisance of himself. I'm quite capable of looking after myself, you know. I don't need someone like him to follow me around.'

'Oh.' Kate looked crestfallen. 'I thought it was rather good of him to offer, that's all. I know he shouldn't have been in the cinema, but he *did* say how sorry and embarrassed he was . . .'

'He *would*, wouldn't he?' snapped Nina. 'Let's stop all this gossip and go and relieve Mr Nicholson of his clips, shall we?'

Mr Nicholson had had his gastric ulcer treated by the removal of part of the ulcerated part of his stomach in a partial gastrectomy. It was a common enough operation but still quite a major one, and he had required intensive nursing in the first few days after coming back from the theatre. Now he was much better, and he quite happily lay back while Nina demonstrated how to remove the metal clips that held the edges of the wound together. 'It's very neat,' he commented. 'Why don't they use stitches like they used to?'

'They still do for many operations, but this is quicker and neater, and you're not overweight, so the surgeon decided to use clips instead,' Nina explained, watching as Kate carefully used the special forceps to spring open the clips.

'And how do you know that when you take away the last one it won't all open up again?' Mr Nicholson asked with morbid curiosity.

'You've got another layer of stitches deeper inside—what we call subcutaneous stitches. They'll dissolve gradually as the wound heals. And look,' she said, swabbing down the area and pressing the scar very lightly, 'it's already healed quite well.

Well done, Kate. Would you like to dress it now?'

Kate deposited the contaminated forceps and clips on the bottom tray of the trolley and went to wash her hands again, just in case she'd touched anything dirty during the procedure.

'When do you reckon they'll let me out?' Mr Nicholson asked. 'I've a job to get back to, you know, Sister.'

Nina smiled. The people who tended to develop gastric ulcers were the hard-working, conscientious types who couldn't bear to be away from their desks for more than a few hours. It was tension and nerves that seemed to lead to the excess production of acid in the stomach, and that in turn led to an ulcer if the patient wasn't careful. Mr Nicholson had only just gone through the long and traumatic experience of his operation and already he was wanting to get back to work!

'That's up to your surgeon, but it should be in the next few days, I'd imagine. You'll need to take it easy for another three weeks, though, Mr Nicholson. No going straight back to work.'

Kate came back to finish the dressing, and as she did so Nina pencilled herself a note to have a few words with Mrs Nicholson when she came to visit this afternoon. Patients sometimes had to do what their wives said, even if they were out of the clutches of the medical staff.

'I'll leave you to it and do a quick ward round,' she said, slipping between the bed curtains. It took quite a time to go round twenty-eight patients, having a few words with them all, checking a pulse here and a fluid chart there.

'Why have I got this big sign above my bed?' one elderly man wanted to know when she stopped to have a chat.

'Didn't the nurse explain when she put it up?' Nina quizzed.

'She said something about me not having any lunch,' he muttered, 'but I didn't understand.'

'The sign says Nil By Mouth,' Nina explained, getting it down so that he could see it for himself. 'You're off to the operating theatre tomorrow morning, aren't you, Mr Glazier?' He nodded. 'Well, for twenty-four hours before you have your operation you mustn't have anything to eat.'

'Nothing at all?' he asked, obviously shocked.

'Nothing at all,' Nina emphasised. 'It may seem tough now, but the anaesthetist won't be able to do his job properly if you've got anything in your stomach. You don't want any complications, do you?' He shook his head. 'You can have as much to drink as you want until . . .' she consulted the sheet of operation times that she was carrying, 'eight o'clock this evening, so you can have some clear soup for lunch. But after eight that's it, I'm afraid. We can't even allow you to have a drink.'

'Not even a cup of tea first thing?' he asked pathetically.

Nina looked sympathetic. 'Not even that. I'm sorry, Mr Glazier, believe me, but it's the best way of ensuring that the operation goes smoothly.'

'In that case,' he said, opening his bedside

locker, 'you can have these. If I get hungry and they're here I'll eat them, I know I will.' And he handed her a big plastic bag full of loose sweets and a bunch of bananas.

'I'll make sure that you have them back just as soon as you're out of the anaesthetic,' Nina promised. 'Though it will be a few days before you fancy them, I'm sure!'

Back in the office she labelled the fruit and sweets and locked them in the cupboard in which patients' valuables were kept. She was just sitting down to get on with some of the backlog of work when there was a knock at the door, and James Farris walked in. He was dressed casually in well-washed jeans and a neatly striped navy and bottle green shirt. These kind of clothes suited him much more than the suits he usually wore, Nina thought unconsciously as she greeted him with a frosty hello. He was an outdoors sort of man, Mr Farris. And he was fit too. His suits, with their padded shoulders and square lines, concealed the fact that his shoulders were quite broad and muscular enough to do without padding. His stomach was trim and flat too, she noted as he sat down in his jeans. They weren't skin-tight by any means, but they did underline the fact that he wasn't a seven-stone weakling.

'I'm off duty,' he said, confused by her perusal of his clothing. 'Did you see the paper? We got off pretty lightly, didn't we? And the TV people only showed a clip of Angie. I didn't hear the radio report, but apparently it mentioned the picket almost in passing and went on to discuss nurses' pay and violence in hospitals.'

Nina gave a snort of disgust. 'So you and Colin Sturgis can sleep easy in your beds again, I suppose? And am I and the other nurses expected just to forget what happened?'

James took a deep breath and counted to ten. Whatever happened, he'd promised himself, he was't going to give her the satisfaction of making him lose his temper. Deciding that it was his best policy to change the subject, he fished around in one of his pockets and held out a key. 'Here you are.' Nina took it, unsure of what it was for. It was warm where it had been tucked up against his body, and she put it down hurriedly on the desk top.

'What's that for?' she asked, nonplussed.

'The key to my house. The key to your flat is in the door.'

'You can have it back,' she said, almost throwing it at him. 'I don't want it.'

'Keep it.' He stood up to go. 'I've come all the way out here to give it to you and I intend you to have it. Technically you're not supposed to have access until you've actually bought the flat, but I can see no reason why you shouldn't have a chance to bring in some of your things, put up a few shelves, that kind of thing, before you move in for good.' He placed the key firmly on her desk and turned to go out. Nina snatched it up again and, without thinking, tried to insert it in his back pocket. Her hand came hard up against his denim-covered buttock and, stunned, she paused

—which gave him time to swing round, out of her grasp.

'Hands off, Sister Newington,' he said with an amused smile. And before she could stop him and tell him that she wouldn't touch him with a barge pole, not if he was the last man on earth, he had gone, striding nonchalantly up the corridor.

Nina's face was hot and her hand was hot too. She hurried out to the basin in the prep room and washed thoroughly, as if soap and water would take away the sudden surge of physical interest she had felt for him. She found herself almost sobbing as she stood over the basin, nailbrush in hand. Why, oh, why did James Farris have to come to *this* hospital? And why did he have to be nice to her, so that she couldn't just despise him as she could most of the other men she met? And why, she cursed, scrubbing her nails until they were pink and angry-looking, did her own body and her own wayward thoughts let her down when he was around? Men didn't interest her, not in that way, anyway. Men were fine as patients, fine when they were ill or feeble, fine in a professional capacity. But not as friends or lover, not after what Alan Gill had done to her.

Kate stood in the doorway and watched her. 'Are you all right, Sister?'

'Yes, of course I am,' Nina asserted briskly. 'My Biro sprang a leak and I'd got black ink all over me. I haven't got any on my face, have I?' she asked, turning to Kate in the full knowledge that she hadn't.

'Nope,' Kate confirmed, and laughed. Nina laughed too. There was only one way to deal with men, and that was to laugh at them too.

The rest of the day passed slowly. Mr Glazier watched longingly as Sunday lunch of roast beef and Yorkshire pudding was dished up, and Nina felt so sorry for him that she asked if he'd like to be transferred to a side ward, where the smell was less tempting. After that there were the usual medicine rounds and bedpans and checks on temperature and pulse, followed by visitors. Nina managed to intercept Mrs Nicholson as she passed the office and made a point of emphasising how well Mr Nicholson was doing—but also how much rest and care he was going to require. 'I know,' said the woman, shaking her head. 'I've told him, of course, that he's going to have three weeks at home. I've told his boss that too, and it's all right as far as he's concerned. But George does fret when he's not able to work. He's a sales representative, Sister, and to people in that line, time is money. Every minute he spends in here he thinks of as lost commission. He's so conscientious he works all hours, you know.'

'Well, if he doesn't slow down he's going to be in serious trouble,' Nina warned. 'If the worst comes to the worst his doctor will have to arrange for him to go away to convalesce, so that he can't even think of going back to work.'

Mrs Nicholson obviously didn't like the sound of that.

'He'd never go,' she said simply. 'There's no one

more stubborn than him, I can assure you.'

'In which case we'll just have to make sure that he has a quiet two weeks at home with you before he goes back to work. Don't worry, Mrs Nicholson, we'll get something sorted out,' Nina promised.

At twenty past three, just forty minutes before she was due to go off duty for the day, the call came from Accident and Emergency. 'We've got a case of acute peritonitis here for you,' announced the duty officer.

'No, you haven't,' retorted Nina. 'I don't have a spare bed. Honest, we're full.'

'Damn!' The duty officer thought for a moment. 'I've tried the other surgical wards and none of them will have him either. Is there anyone you can move, Sister Newington? You're our last resort.'

Nina had a think. She didn't want Mr Glazier moved, not the night before his operation. There was Mr Palmer, who'd had his kneecap removed and ought by rights to be in Orthopaedic. 'I have one patient, Palmer . . .' she explained the situation. 'If you can get him transferred then I'll take this emergency.'

'Righty-ho,' came the duty officer's voice down the line. 'Consider it done. He's in a bad way, so we're sending him up now rather than keeping him down here. If you'd prep him . . .'

'OK.' Nina reached for her notepad. 'What time is he due in theatre?'

'About an hour, I'd say,' came the reply. 'We're still trying to round up an anaesthetist. The duty anaesthetist's got a Caesarian section coming up in the next few minutes.'

'How about the surgeon? Has he seen him?' asked Nina.

'Yes, just quickly. It's the new man, Mr Farris.'

'Oh,' said Nina flatly.

'He's all right, actually,' said the duty officer, quite misunderstanding her. 'I've heard he's rather good. He'll be up soon after the patient, just to do another examination before he goes to scrub up. Expect him when you see him.'

Ten minutes later the emergency admission arrived. Kate and the staff nurse had hurriedly bundled Mr Palmer's belongings into a bag and helped him into a wheelchair, which was stationed at the far end of the ward, where patients were watching the sport on the TV. He accepted the change calmly. After ten days on a hectic surgical ward he had seen how rapidly decisions and changes could be made. With as much speed as could be mustered. The empty bed was brought to the position nearest the nurses' desk at the top of the ward where the night staff would be able to keep a close eye on it. Nina herself helped Kate to whip off the sheets and replace them with clean ones after only the briefest sponge down of the plastic mattress cover. They were just finishing layering the pale blue blankets, which had MOORSIDE printed across them in orange letters, to deter any laundry thieves, when the porters arrived with the patient. His notes were handed over and he was lifted carefully on to the bed. Gentle though they were, he still groaned when they touched him.

Nina looked through the notes. There wasn't much information. 'Mr Haslett?' He looked at her through eyes narrowed with pain. 'We're going to prepare you to go down to the operating theatre so that we can sort your problem out. The surgeon will be here in a minute to give you a pre-med, which will help you with the pain.'

He nodded painfully at her, but didn't look very confident. 'It's all right.' She took his wrist and felt for his pulse, which was sluggish. 'You're going to be OK now.' She smiled at him as warmly as she could. When people were frightened and in pain it was sometimes difficult to know what to say to comfort them.

'I wish you'd speak to me like that,' murmured James as he took the man's wrist from her fingers. He gave her a dancing glance of amusement.

'*Nothing* would make me speak to you like that,' she muttered as she turned back to the trolley. 'You'll want a naso-gastric tube, won't you, Mr Farris?' she added with saccharine sweetness as she offered the equipment for him to insert. James took it without a word and began the long and unpleasant process of persuading a distressed patient to swallow the tube which had been inserted in his nostril.

Nina watched him, helping to support Mr Haslett as he was turned in the appropriate way. She quite liked the calm way in which he talked to the patient. There was no side, no attempt to make himself seem important. Many consultants, even when dealing with children or the very old, liked to remain distant and remote and rather overbearing. Not so James, who perched on the edge of the bed, his jeans and casual shirt visible under a hastily flung on white coat.

'Good.' He stood up and went to wash his hands. 'Now, Sister.' There was an invisible iciness under the title. 'I'd like a consent form from your office, please. And while you're there please call down to the theatre and find out whether we've got an anaesthetist yet. If we have, get him up here immediately to do the pre-med. I'd also like the patient catheterised and the contents of his stomach aspirated. Clean him up as much as you can before he comes down.'

'Of course,' Nina said smartly, as if these instructions were an insult to her professional competence. 'What's the problem?'

'No idea.' James ran his hand distractedly through his hair, keeping his voice down so that it wouldn't travel. 'I've had a look at his X-rays and they give very little indication. It's a case of going in there and having a poke round. Could be a ruptured appendix or a perforation of the duodenum —or anything else, for that matter.'

'Right I'll warn the next shift.' Nina jotted down the note on the pad that she carried with her. Peritonitis cases required pretty intensive nursing. They could take nothing by mouth for several days after the operation, they received heavy doses of antibiotics, and they were often kept sedated for the first few days. There would be a drain inserted into their abdomen to drain off the infected fluids within the peritoneal cavity, and there had to be hourly tests of their stomach contents and blood to check whether the poisoning—because that in effect was what it was—was spreading. All this meant a lot of routine work for the nurses. In fact a couple of cases like this could tie up a nurse's whole working day, leaving the others to cope with the less intensive demands of the other patients. If Intensive Care had a spare bed they could often be persuaded to take such a case for the first few days—but a spare bed in Intensive Care was a very rare phenomenon.

There was no time to make the various processes the patient had to be put through very dignified. He was in pain and some danger, and they had to prepare him as best they could for surgery. 'Do you think it'll be all right?' he asked Nina after he had been washed and shaved from neck to knee, as was standard for abdominal surgery.

'Yes!' she smiled as brightly as she could. 'You're going to feel awful for the next few days, Mr Haslett, though we'll do all we can for you. But give it a week or two and you'll be right as rain.'

'That surgeon seemed a bit young to know what he was doing,' Mr Haslett gasped as she gave him the dose of pethidine that had been prescribed by the anaesthetist.

'I've heard he's very competent,' Nina said comfortingly. It was like having to play devil's advocate. First the duty officer and now the patient. The problem with James Farris was that in the blinkered eyes of most of the people in this hospital he was too good to be true. The pethidine began to take effect and she saw his body begin to relax as the pain abated. 'Don't worry,' was her parting remark. 'You're in very good hands.'

He was too, she had to admit grudgingly. Damn it. Damn James Farris and his interfering ways! If I were a fatalist, she thought as she prepared her report for the next shift, I'd say that we were destined to collide, like the *Titanic* and the iceberg. The flat; the cinema; the way she didn't seem to be able to put him off, no matter what she said and did. It might be nice, a little voice somewhere in the back of her head whispered, to take a chance and get to know him. After all, if it was fate there was no way she could sidestep it. 'Don't be ridiculous,' she said aloud to her reflection in Sister Parker's mirror, tucked out of sight behind the filing cabinet. Men were not to be trusted. Men were flippant and selfish, they walked all over women if they were given the chance. And James Farris was definitely not going to get a chance to walk all over her.

CHAPTER FIVE

'I'M BORED,' said Anna, switching off the TV set just as Rock Hudson and Doris Day kissed and the credits of the film began to roll. 'Do you want to go for a walk? How about going somewhere for a drink?'

Nina, who was on her hands and knees packing her records, looked up. 'Monteverdi, Trini Lopez and the Sex Pistols. Yours or mine?' She waved three albums at Anna, who looked at them curiously.

'I've no idea. Never seen them before.'

'I don't remember them,' shrugged Nina.

'You have them,' they both chorused together, and both looked appalled at the idea of owning them.

'Something else for the Oxfam bag,' laughed Nina, putting them aside. 'Oxfam aren't going to know what's hit them when they suddenly receive half the contents of this flat!' Both girls were packing their things up in readiness for their moves, Anna to London and Nina to Arcadia Gardens.

'Did you see the solicitor?' Anna asked idly.

'Yes. The search is OK and so is the land registry. With a bit of luck we'll complete at the end of the week after next. It's very quick, but then there's no chain of people waiting for each other.'

Anna massaged her toes. 'I wish I could see this place of yours. Why don't we walk round there this evening? It's nice out and you've been in all day. I bet you could do with some fresh air.'

Nina hesitated. She had been back to have a look at the flat twice, but only when she was absolutely certain that James Farris wouldn't be at home. She had actually nipped down to Theatres to check his schedule, which had raised a few eyebrows. Nursing Sisters weren't normally to be found prowling around outside the theatre suites. Colin Sturgis had caught her and asked if she was looking for anyone, and she had had to lie and say that she'd come to check the schedule for one of her patients. He had looked at her as if she was completely crazy—after all, there were well-tried channels for getting information like that—but hadn't made any further comment. She looked out of the window now. It was a warm evening, slightly breezy, and after a day spent rummaging through the contents of her cupboards and shelves she felt like getting out. James, she knew, played squash or went down to the hospital social club most evenings. She knew because he'd mentioned it and asked why he didn't see her there, to which she had replied that she saw quite enough of the hospital's staff at work, thanks, and didn't feel the need to spend the evening watching them sweat it out on the squash court or chat each other up in the bar. Kate had said something too, about having a chat with him when she went down there. She had been surprised that he didn't seem to be attached to anyone. Nina had noticed how Kate talked more often these days of the social club. Perhaps she had stepped up her attendance in the hope of getting to know Mr Farris better?

'We can walk over there if you want,' she told Anna now, annoyed by that final thought. Who cared if he was at home or not? She had a perfect right to take a look at *her* home if she wanted. 'And we can even go in, if you want. I've got a key. The guy who owns it says I can take some things round and do any decorating that I want.'

Anna looked surprised. 'Why didn't you say? You know I've been dying to take a look at it! If we're going over there now, why don't we fill the car up and take these boxes with us?'

Nina mulled it over. Yes, that way if he *was* there it wouldn't look as if she and Anna were just out snooping. An hour later Anna's battered Renault 5 turned into Arcadia Gardens and stopped conveniently outside the house, but just as they got out a strange man hailed them. Anna looked at him, puzzled, for a moment, then greeted him warmly. 'Nina, Nina!' she called excitedly. Nina emerged from the rear of the car, where she had just opened the hatch to retrieve an old eggbox full of kitchen utensils. 'This is . . .' And she introduced him as an old college friend.

Nina had intended to spend a while in the flat with Anna, showing her all the merits of the new place and slowly carrying boxes and bags upstairs. As it was, the entire contents of the car were dumped on the floor of her bedroom within ten minutes of arriving, Anna's friend being most efficient when it came to lugging boxes up long flights of stairs.

Anna looked at her apologetically. 'Would you mind much if we went off for a drink? I can come and have a look at the flat later, can't I, if you've got a key?'

Nina looked at the pair of them, obviously quite desperate to find a quiet corner so that they could discuss old times. 'You two go for a drink, by all means, but I think I'll stay here and unpack a few bits and pieces,' she said tactfully.

'You don't mind?' Anna felt suddenly guilty.

'No, of course not!' It was said with more cheerfulness than she actually felt, and she accompanied them downstairs and let them out of the front door. There was one last box, full of odds and ends of books and records and souvenirs collected over the years, waiting at the bottom of the stairs. She had just picked it up and was about to embark on her final assault on the stairs when the front door opened again and James came into the hall. He was wearing white shorts and a T-shirt, and he had his squash racket tucked into the bag he held under one arm.

'Hello there.' He showed no surprise at finding her standing in his hall. 'Do you need a hand with that?' Nina tried not to let her gaze keep dipping to his knees. His legs were tanned and covered with golden hair—not that she cared less what his legs were like, of course. It was just that she wasn't used to seeing him in shorts, she told herself.

Reader Service
FREEPOST
P O Box 236
Croydon
Surrey
CR9 9EL

THIS IS YOUR CLAIM CARD
Post it free today.

YES! Please send me my two FREE Masquerade novels, along with my free diamond zirconia necklace and mystery gift.

Please also reserve a Reader Service subscription for me, so that I can enjoy 4 brand new Masquerade novels every other month for only £6 delivered to my home, postage and packing free.

If I decide not to subscribe, I shall write to you within 10 days and owe nothing. The 2 free books and 2 free gifts will be mine to keep in any case.

I understand that I may cancel or suspend my subscription at any time simply by writing to you. I am over 18 years of age.

(Please write in BLOCK CAPITALS)

YOURS FREE

This diamond
zirconia necklace

Name _____

Address _____

_____ Postcode _____

Signature _____

mps

NA7MA

'No, no. I'm quite all right,' she muttered hurriedly.

He smiled. 'Is there anything else I can do? Now I come to think of it, I don't remember putting any lightbulbs in the fittings. Shall I get a couple from down here and bring them up for you? It'll only take me a minute.'

'There's no need. I'm not staying long,' Nina lied, cursing her own stupidity for not having thought of lightbulbs herself. It would have been so much more satisfying simply to tell him that she'd done it herself.

'Well,' he shrugged, 'if you need any help I'm here.'

'I *don't* need any help,' she said loftily, climbing the first few stairs. 'And even if I did, I don't need you. I've got a friend upstairs and he can fix anything I need doing.' She subtly emphasised the 'he'.

'Oh, I see.' The smile faded from James's face.

Nina looked down at the box she was carrying. She needed something substantial to persuade James that he really wasn't necessary. On the top of the pile of books was *Now We Are Six*, a favourite book of hers as a child. She had brought her copy with her when she had left home, and now it was coming with her to her new place. 'Milne,' she lurched.

'What?' James, too far beneath her to see the book, didn't understand.

'My friend upstairs. Dr Milne.' Nina felt her throat go dry. She wasn't very good at deceptions like these. Stuck behind the books were a couple of records she'd found lurking in a cupboard, and the familiar face of Bruce Springsteen peeped from an album cover. 'Bruce—Bruce Milne. Dr Bruce Milne. That's his name.'

'Oh, right.' James reflected for a moment. 'Is he at Moorside? I don't think I've met him.'

'Er—no.' Nina inserted it so quickly that she felt sure it looked suspicious. 'No, he's at the County Hospital in York.'

'Ah.' James smiled the kind of ungrudging smile of a man who has just come second in a race. He seemed to shrink an inch or two, and he folded his arms defensively across his chest as she turned away and walked up the stairs.

Nina felt a surge of pleasure at having deflated him so utterly—and it was swiftly followed by another surge of self-disgust that she could so openly mislead him. Never mind, Bruce Milne was a useful ally to have at such a time. She thought about his personality as she climbed. He'd be a leading cancer specialist. And he'd be six foot tall, with sandy hair and legs . . . No, she corrected herself, that wouldn't do. He'd be very dark, with flashing grey eyes like a *real* romantic hero. He'd drive an old sports car—nothing too brash, and he'd have a house looking over the river in York. That would do. And of course, he'd be very broadminded, a New Man of the kind that feminists dream about. He'd cook and wash and enjoy having her female friends round to dinner. He'd allow her to pay her own way when they went out. But he'd also have a romantic streak and occasionally stun her by buying roses or whisking her off to Paris for the weekend. Nina chuckled to herself. Whoever found such a man could count herself extremely lucky. Well, Bruce Milne, the invisible doctor, would be *her* perfect man.

Nina pushed the door of her flat, expecting it to open. It didn't, and the box she was carrying bruised her ribs. She shoved again, less gently this time. Then she put the box down. This was too much! The last person out of the flat, either Anna or her friend, had shut the door behind them, little suspecting that the key was lying on top of the boxes in the sitting-room. Now the Yale lock had snapped shut. She was locked out of her own home.

For five minutes she sat on the top step of the stairs and pondered what to do. She could call a locksmith—except that her bag was locked in the flat with her purse. She couldn't go back home because Anna wouldn't be there—and her key was in her bag, with her purse, which was locked in the flat . . . She shook her head as she ran through the possibilities. There was, of course, only one possible answer to the problem, but it was an answer she didn't want to have to resort to. James might have a spare key. And if he didn't, he might have a screwdriver or something so that she could get in. She sat there for another five minutes, steeling herself to go down and ask. How could she have been so stupid? Why hadn't she immediately pocketed the key so that this didn't happen? She just couldn't go down and ask him to help her, she couldn't!

The light began to fade, and when she stood up to

look out of the window halfway up the final flight of stairs she could see the sun sinking behind the rooftops of the houses on the opposite side of the road. Well, she couldn't sit up here all night, she thought miserably. It seemed a long way down the two flights of stairs, and at each step she felt like turning and running back up again. Finally she found herself in the hall, with James's white-painted front door waiting for her knock. She rapped her knuckles against it and waited. Nothing happened. She knocked again harder, because the idea of him not being there was more worrying than the prospect of being alone and shut out and helpless.

Suddenly, just as she was about to knock for a third time, the door was opened. James stood there in a towel, his hair damp. He was rubbing at it with another towel. 'Hallo,' he said with mild surprise. 'Is everything all right up there?'

Nina tried to stop her eyes from wandering down his torso, from his broad shoulders with their light tan and scattering of golden freckles down to the point where a line of golden hair ran down the centre of his belly and mercifully disappeared into the mossy green towel he wore around his hips. He was one of those naturally muscular men, she noted. Not all bulging biceps but with a broad and well-defined chest . . . She swallowed. 'I seem to be locked out of my flat.' Her voice was high-pitched, like Minnie Mouse's. She gulped again. 'Do you have a spare key??'

'What about your friend Dr Milne? Isn't he up

there?' James ran his fingers through his damp hair, sweeping it back off his forehead. Nina hated him all the more. How could he? Instead of apologising for being in this state of undress he was deliberately standing here and taunting her.

'He had to go,' she stated bluntly. 'Look, all I want to know is whether you've got a spare key.'

James shook his head. 'I put it on the draining board in your kitchen so that you'd find it when you came. I didn't want you to think I was keeping my own key to your place. I don't want to invade your privacy.' Nina could have hit him. Why had he been so stupidly thoughtful? If he'd kept the duplicate he could have given it to her right now, instead of which she was well and truly locked out. 'Come in a minute while I put some clothes on,' he said after a moment's thought. 'I can probably break into the place somehow.' He didn't look very pleased with her; but then, Nina thought guiltily, he had no reason to be. She'd told him he wasn't wanted and now here she was, having dragged him from the shower by the looks of things, asking him to help her break into her own flat.

'Thanks,' she muttered under her breath, feeling ungracious all the while. But damn it, she wasn't going to fawn all over him like some silly little woman who needed assistance to put in a lightbulb. He led her through to the sitting room. It was big and comfortable, decorated in shades of grey and terracotta, with large old pieces of antique furniture mixing with a huge sofa and a wall covered almost entirely in bookshelves.

'I'll only be a minute,' he promised with a wry smile, and left her. Nina heard his footsteps as he ran up the stairs. She looked round enviously. The ceiling of the room was high, with a big bay window looking out over the leafy front garden. There was an ornate plaster cornice and a big pine fireplace. She thought of her own little flat up in the eaves—it must have been the servants' quarters. She looked along the mantelpiece for clues about its owner's life. There were a couple of invitations to parties in London, a foot carved out of black granite, probably very old, a funny-looking bird made out of red clay and a photo in a simple glass frame of a girl with beautiful long blonde hair. Nina picked it up and looked at it more closely. Trust him to have a girlfriend like that—all blonde and tanned and sweetly pretty in her summer dress. That, of course, was exactly the sort of woman he'd go for. The kind who wouldn't say boo to a goose.

'All right?' She'd been so absorbed in looking at the photo that she hadn't heard James return. Now he stood behind her, only a few inches away. When he saw what she was looking at, his expression froze. 'Inspecting my belongings, I see,' he commented icily.

Nina placed the picture back on the mantelpiece and tried not to feel guilty. She wasn't snooping. People walked into her flat and looked at the things left on display there, and she didn't feel hurt about that. 'I like the foot,' she said calmly, wondering whether he was miffed because she wasn't supposed to know about his girlfriend.

'It's Egyptian,' he said offhandedly, refusing to look her in the eye. 'It's all that remains of a statue of Rameses the Second.' Nina was quietly impressed. It was more interesting than the kind of ornaments or bits and pieces that most people collected. And actually owning something, anything, that old appealed to her. 'Let's get that door opened,' James said clumsily, turning away from her and leading her out. It was as if he didn't want her there in his home, and Nina felt chastened. Because despite all that she'd said and thought about him, it suddenly dawned on her that she would have liked to have spent more time with him there. She had made it perfectly plain to him that she didn't want him around. Now the boot was on the other foot and he was showing her out, making it plain that he didn't want her snooping in his sitting-room, and she wondered whether he had felt the kind of hurt she felt stab her now. Part of her wanted to say sorry, and the other independent part of her wished she didn't have to have anything to do with him at all. And somehow that fiercely independent bit of her always won, even if it left her feeling guilty.

'I'll try to get in using this.' James rummaged through his wallet, which he took from a jacket hanging from the hallstand. 'If it doesn't work we'll have to force it open and repair it afterwards.' He held up a plastic credit card. 'I once locked myself out when I was a student, and it worked that time.'

Nina said nothing. What could she say? Sorry —for the inconvenience, for taking up his time . . .

But he'd offered to help her, hadn't he? She gritted her teeth and followed him upstairs. She hated begging favours of anyone; it was a sign of weakness to go running to someone else when things went wrong, and she hated herself for allowing things to get out of her control. It gave him the upper hand. Having helped her out once he'd expect her to help him out in future. What she really wanted was not to be bothered by him at all.

All these thoughts ran through her head as James stood on her little landing and slipped the smooth plastic of the credit card between the door and the frame at the height of the lock. She stood back on the stairs to give him light. Anyway, she didn't want to have to get too close to him. He smelt tantalisingly of soap and clean hair. She looked at his strong masculine feet as he wiggled the credit card about. It would be very easy to get involved with this man, but she wasn't going to do it. She wasn't going to risk her independence or compromise her ideals just for the sake of a few days or weeks of pleasure with James Farris.

He gave a grunt and pushed the door. It opened easily. *'Voilà!'* he exclaimed, straightening his back. 'If I ever want to leave medicine I've obviously got a great future in housebreaking!'

Nina smiled. 'Thanks.' It sounded very grudging. Before she could stop him, he bent and picked up the box of books and records and bits that she had left lying by the door.

'Where do you want these?' he asked, nudging the door open even wider with his knee.

'It's all right, I can do it,' she insisted, but he ignored her and walked in, shoving open the door of the kitchen and depositing the box on one of the worktops. Nina followed him in, peeved. She hadn't invited him in. It was her flat and she didn't want him here . . . She was brought up short by a row of scarlet geraniums sitting along the window-sill. They matched the red trimmings of the units and looked quite stunning. 'What are these doing here?' she queried.

James turned to her, handing her a white envelope. 'I bought some for a couple of planters I was making in the garden, but they were too bright. I thought they'd look good in here, though, so I brought them up.'

'Well, you can take them back down again!' Nina snapped. She knew it was wrong; she knew she ought to say thank you, but she couldn't, because she knew that if she began giving in to him on anything at all he would have won their battle. 'I don't want anything from you, nothing at all. Can't you understand that?'

James's eyes expressed his surprise and annoyance. He'd bought the plants because he'd thought she'd like them. He knew she liked bright colours, and he'd imagined she would be pleased. 'No,' he said flatly. 'I thought they'd please you. They're just a gesture—my way of saying welcome to your new home.' His voice was icy. 'You can't say you want nothing from me—you've just asked me to come up here and open your door for you. I don't mind doing it,' he went on, ignoring her attempt to silence him, 'but you might force yourself to be nice about it instead of constantly snapping at me.'

'Is that what the flowers are for—so that I'll "be nice" to you?' demanded Nina, sweeping one of them into the sink. The pot smashed against the stainless steel and a flower head tumbled to the floor. James silently picked up the pieces of clay and tried to rescue the plant. He was furious, she could see that from way in which one of the muscles at the side of his jaw ticked away. 'You've got a nerve, walking in here as if you own the place——'

'I *do* own the place,' James inserted quietly.

'——telling me what to do and what not to do. Does your girlfriend know about all this? Porn films and flowers for the nurses?'

Not for the first time she wondered if she'd goaded him too far. It would be so easy for him to lash out and floor her, and he was obviously angry enough to do so if he'd been inclined. 'I don't have a girlfriend.' His voice was so still and quiet that Nina almost strained to catch the words. 'I don't make a habit of watching dirty films. And I wouldn't dream of having anything to do with a woman who'd be nice to me for the price of six geraniums.' He pushed the white envelope into her hands. 'Here's your spare key. You'd better keep it safe somewhere so that this doesn't happen again.'

Nina took it numbly and James pushed past her, out of the kitchen. 'I'm sorry. Look, I just . . .'

He halted and turned back to her. 'That's the first time you've said sorry to me. Maybe it's a good sign. Perhaps you're not quite as paranoid as I'd diagnosed.' He put his head to one side in a questioning attitude. 'If things go on improving like this we might even be able to have a normal friendly relationship—in twenty years' time.' He turned to go, but she flew at him, grabbing him by the arm and forcing him to turn round again.

'*I'm* not paranoid! Just because I don't behave like all the other little nurses who've no doubt thrown themselves at you since you arrived at Moorside.' Her eyebrows were jammed firmly together in a black line. 'Your problem is that you're not used to independent women. You think we should all rely on you—you fancy yourself as the strong macho type, don't you?' the words tumbled out without any thought. 'You wouldn't know how to treat a liberated woman,' she spat accusingly.

'Yes, I would.' James grabbed her by the shoulders and for a moment she thought he was going to shake her hard. Then, 'Like this,' he muttered, and catching her chin with one hand he kissed her, kissed her hard, so that she took a step backwards and found herself jammed against the sink unit. 'There,' he murmured, lifting his lips from hers. 'It worked, didn't it?' His eyes were gentle. He had obviously enjoyed it—and he obviously intended to do it again, Nina realised as he bent back towards her. Remembering what she and Anna had learned in their self-defence lessons at the women's centre, she raised her hand and brought it down firmly on his nose, managing simultaneously to knee him in the groin. With a startled cry he doubled up, both hands clutching the injured parts.

'You're damned lucky I don't call the police now and tell them you tried to rape me,' she said, suddenly cool and calculating.

James's face was pale, except for the red line across the bridge of his nose. 'I hadn't realised you hated men so much,' he gasped.

Nina glared at him. 'That's typical, isn't it? Just because I don't want you all over me and I put you in your place you tell me I'm a man-hater! Well, I've got some news for you, Mr Farris,' she added, her mind racing. 'I won't be living here alone in a fortnight's time. I'll be living with a man, Dr Bruce Milne. And he certainly doesn't think I'm a man-hater!'

James looked at her. How could any woman look so attractive and yet be so vindictive? After their first couple of encounters he had come to the conclusion that she was probably aggressive because of some unhappy relationship she'd had in the past. He had thought that with time and patience and understanding he would be able to wear down her defences. But this news meant something he hadn't even contemplated. If she had a relationship with another man that meant that it wasn't men in general she disliked; it meant simply that she had something personal against *him*. It was like being doused with a bucket of cold water. All the time he'd been kidding himself that if he could win her confidence they could get on well together. He'd even thought that he'd been helping her. Now it looked as if it was something purely personal. He might as well give up.

'I wish Dr Milne the best of luck,' he said coldly. 'He's a braver man than me.' And, leaving her speechless, he made his way, hobbling, downstairs.

CHAPTER SIX

'Is THAT Mr Boxer back from Theatre already?'
Nina checked her watch. 'They're really getting
through it this morning! Put him over there,' she
instructed the porter and the nurse who was holding his transfusion bottle. 'I'll be with you myself in
two minutes. Nurse Osborne, would you give a
hand with Mr Boxer?'

Operating days were always hectic, but today
was even more chaotic than usual. One of the staff
nurses who should have come on duty at eight had
simply failed to turn up, and so they were short-
handed. They had two intensive nursing cases, one
of whom was Mr Haslett, the emergency peritonitis. Although James Farris had discovered the
cause of the problem and operated to relieve it, he
was still very ill and the drugs that Nina was administering didn't seem to be fighting the infection
with much success.

'Sister!' Helen Osborne trotted across the ward.
'It's Mr Angelou. His pulse is very fast.' Nina
followed her to the bedside and took the patient's
pulse herself. Yes, it was regular but very fast—not
a good sign after surgery.

'Stay with him, Helen. It's probably only sinus
tachycardia. I'll get Mr Nash and we'll put up an
infusion while we wait for him.' Helen nodded.

This problem could be due to a number of causes
—anaemia and pain among them—but any
arrhythmia after an operation could be serious.
The last thing they needed this morning was a
cardiac arrest.

Using the telephone at the nurses' station, she
made the call down to Theatre. If Mr Nash was in
the middle of an op he'd nominate a houseman to
come up to the ward for him. He *was* unable to
come, as she'd suspected, and she called down to
the switchboard to locate Tony Brewer, his houseman. From there the switchboard would activate
his bleeper, and with a bit of luck he would be here
in ten minutes or so. At that moment one of the
other staff nurses came hurrying over with news of
another post-operative patient who was experienc-
ing breathing difficulty, and instead of giving a
hand with Mr Boxer or going back to check with
Helen on Mr Angelou, Nina had to go down to the
end of the ward. On days like this, with relatives
calling up to find out how patients were faring and
beds being trundled in and out of the ward every
few minutes, or so it seemed, she wished she could
split herself up into a dozen different people.

Dr Brewer was at Mr Angelou's bedside when
she came back. He was young and brash, a loud-
mouthed type who seemed to have slipped into
medicine while everyone had their eyes shut. Nina
had met him soon after he had arrived at the
hospital and he had strung her a whole line about
working hard and living harder—which, from what
she could make out, meant that he drove his car too

fast and was frequently to be found the worse for wear in the hospital sports and social club bar. His conquests among the nursing staff were legendary. To anyone over the age of twenty-one he was a bit of a joke, but with student nurses and the more impressionable staff he had the reputation of being a great catch—which explained why he and Nina had never seen eye to eye and were never likely to. '*Here* you are, Sister,' he commented facetiously when Nina stepped through the bed curtains and into the cubicle. 'At last' was the message inherent in his words. Nina said nothing but proffered the notes while he took pulse and blood pressure details and sounded the patient's heart.

'I don't think there's anything to worry about, Mr Angelou,' he said at last, 'but we'll give you a shot of pain-killer and I'd like us to wire you up to the cardiograph. It sounds worrying, but in fact it's just so that we'll have a visual record of how your heart's behaving. OK, Sister?' Nina nodded and handed him the prescription sheet to update. He scribbled the dose and the drug and handed it back to her. 'Immediately, please, Sister. No hanging about. I've got to go and see a patient on Gower ward, but I'll be back.' And with that he took off.

Helen was sent to get the cardiograph machine from the prep room and to prepare the injection of morphine sulphate, which Tony Brewer had specified on the prescription form. Nina stayed with Mr Angelou, soothing him and telling him what they were going to do. It was Jane who returned a minute or two later with the kidney dish containing a syringe and an ampoule of the morphine. 'Helen's answering the phone, but she asked me to bring you this,' Jane explained. 'In that case you can help me administer it,' Nina instructed. Together they gently rolled Mr Angelou on to his side and eased down his pyjama bottoms to expose the top outer quarter of his buttock. 'Draw up the dose, Jane,' Nina said encouragingly. All the nurses gave injections, and although they didn't administer drugs like morphine without supervision, all were quite capable of doing so.

The bed curtains parted again—it was like Piccadilly Circus, Nina thought reprovingly—and James Farris looked through. 'Hallo, Sister,' he said flatly, without the slightest trace of expression on his face. They had met professionally twice since the scene at Arcadia Gardens the other night, and each time he had treated her as if they barely knew each other. She thought of all she'd said, and of her stupid remark about Bruce Milne, and winced. 'I've come to have a look at Mr Haslett. Do you have five minutes?'

'Sister?' Jane had drawn the morphine into the syringe and was waiting, poised, with it.

'Yes,' Nina nodded, and both Jane and James seemed to take it as their reply, for Jane plunged the needle into Mr Angelou with practised skill and James held back the bed curtain for Nina to slip out. Helen arrived at that moment with the cardiograph, and with a, 'Help Jane with Mr Angelou,'

Nina followed James across to Mr Haslett's bed.

Mr Haslett was lightly sedated, to ensure that he was getting the rest he needed. A drip in his right arm ensured that he was getting the correct balance of fluids and electrolytes. James looked through his notes, paying particular attention to the lab reports. Then he checked his drain, from which infected pus and contaminated material was extracted from the wound in his abdomen. 'He's improving, slowly,' he noted. 'I'm still worried about his temperature, though.' They talked for a few moments, but as strangers. It was impossible to believe that he had kissed her—and even more impossible to believe what she had said to him about Dr Bruce Milne. What had come over her? It was as if, left alone with a man, she panicked and did the most appalling things. They were just discussing alternative forms of treatment for Mr Haslett when a white-faced Jane came rocketing up.

'Sister, Sister, you've got to come. I've made a terrible mistake!'

Nina and James both turned to her. 'What's wrong?' Nina asked. 'Is it Mr Angelou?'

'Yes!' Jane tried to keep her voice down, and Nina steered her away from the patients and towards the nurses' station. James came too, looking concerned. 'I gave Mr Angelou 40 mg of morphine —and it should have been 10 mg. It said 40 mg on the prescription form, but that's far too much. I've just realised,. . .' She wrung her hands.

Nina, who was carrying all the paperwork and files, flicked back to Mr Angelou's details. The prescription form was there. She read it. Without any doubt, it said, in Tony Brewer's handwriting, 'Inj. Morphone sulphate 40 mg.' To her own eye, which had seen thousands of similar instructions before, the 40 looked like the 10 that she would expect to see. 'You're right, Jane,' she said with a sickening thud to her stomach. 'How much did you give him?'

'I gave what it said—40 mg.' Jane looked near to tears. 'Have I killed him?'

'No.' James grabbed the prescription sheet and looked at it himself. 'Didn't it occur to either of you that this is a big dose?'

'Mr Angelou's a big man,' Jane pointed out. 'I just assumed that because he's heavy and because the doctor wanted an immediate effect he'd ordered a large dose. Then I said something in passing to Helen and she said that no one ever prescribes more than 15 mg.'

Nina looked at the prescription sheet again, and felt an overwhelming desire to be sick. Despite that, her outward appearance was calm. 'Look,' she said, showing it again to James. 'I expected to see 10 mg, and if you read it quickly it does look like 10 mg. I didn't query it. But Jane's right, it actually says 40 mg. I might have noticed that it was too much when she drew the injection up, but then you arrived . . .'

'Oh, so it's all *my* fault, is it?' He sighed. 'We've got no time for recriminations now, Sister. 'You've

got a supply of nalorphine on the ward, I hope?'
Nina nodded, tight-lipped and anxious not to show
how worried she was. She put the notes, including
the prescription form, down on the counter of the
nurses' station and hurried to get the key to the
dangerous drugs cupboard. She knew only too well
what was going to happen now. There would be an
inquiry—there always was when a patient was
accidentally given the wrong dose or the wrong
type of medication. Mr Angelou wouldn't die, she
could at least put that out of her thoughts. They'd
caught the error quickly enough, thank goodness.
But it could well mean the end of her short career as
Sister on the ward. She pushed the thought to the
back of her mind. There was nothing she could do
about it now. She must just be as quick and efficient
as possible, to try and make up in some way for the
error.

James was at the patient's bedside, checking his
vital signs. Already Mr Angelou's breathing was
falling in reaction to the huge dose of morphine he
had received. Nina administered oxygen while
James gave the patient a jab of the antidote. They
stood waiting for five minutes in silence, Nina with
her fingers jammed to Mr Angelou's wrist, James
listening to his heartbeat. At last he straightened
up. 'It's all right, his breathing's fine now. You'd
better get someone to keep an eye on him constantly for the next six hours, though. And you'd
better report the incident now, so that no one can
say it was covered up.' He looked at her reprovingly, shaking his head slightly. 'It's appalling how

often this kind of thing happens. There's a rush on in the ward, all the rules go to pot, and then this happens.'

'Things did not go to pot, as you put it!' Nina protested as loudly as she could. No one could know for sure how much a patient was taking in, even when they seemed to be sedated. Some drugs, particularly those administered before an operation, had the effect of making the hearing very keen, and many an apparently comatose patient had been distressed by some casual remark delivered by someone who had thought they were dead to the world. 'Dr Brewer made a major error on his prescription. That's not my fault, you know.'

'For God's sake, Nina,' muttered James. 'you can't go blaming him!'

'Why? Because he's a doctor and I'm just a nurse? Is that it? The fact that he scribbled down the wrong dosage in his illegible scrawl, something that might have been a 10 and might have been a 40—and it's *my* fault!'

'Look, it could have happened to anyone,' James murmured, trying it play it down. 'But the fact is that it's got to be reported and it'll be you, as Ward Sister, who'll have the explaining to do.' He paused. They both waited, expecting someone to enter the cubicle, because there was definitely a figure moving outside. But no one came in and, chastened, Nina went back to the bed and checked Mr Angelou's respiration. He seemed fine—and the racing pulse he had been exhibiting earlier had slowed down pretty much to normal.

'Nina . . .' James tried again. 'Doctors are under
a lot of strain, you must know that. Your,' he
hesitated, looking for the right word. Lover? Boyfriend? No, feminists hated that kind of designa-
tion, didn't they? 'Your friend,' he said carefully,'
Dr Milne, he'll have told you all about the kind of
problems doctors go through.'

Nina looked at him blankly for a moment. In the
chaos of the past twenty minutes she had wiped all
thought of her spur-of-the-moment creation from
her mind. 'You know—Dr Milne, your friend.'
James stared at her curiously. Good lord, the man
was going to move in with her and she didn't even
seem to recognise his name! James couldn't forget
it. Dr Bruce Milne. It had a glamorous kind of ring
about it. Doubtless Dr Milne would be tall and dark
and handsome—and he would also have to be some
kind of a saint, to win the heart of this infuriating
woman.

'Dr Milne,' Nina said scathingly, feeling the
words rising spontaneously to her lips without any
real thought, 'isn't just a run-of-the-mill houseman.
He's a consultant—he's the leading endocrinologist in the whole of Yorkshire.' She could scarcely
believe her own ears at this. Since when had the
invisible doctor been an endocrinologist? And
wasn't it a bit dangerous to start making these kind
of boasts? 'What's more,' she went on for good
measure, 'I don't think he'd agree with you that
doctors can be excused their mistakes because
they're under stress. So am I, particularly on days
like these. You can't expect me to be everywhere at

once, doing everything on the ward. And simply because a member of your own fraternity has fouled up you shouldn't band together to protect him.'

'I'm not doing that,' James protested.

'Oh yes, you are.' Nina drew back the bed curtains and motioned Helen to come over and keep an eye on the patient. 'He's stable, but I'd like fifteen-minute checks.' Her eyes strayed to the nurses' station, just a few yards away. Tony Brewer was standing at the counter scribbling on a sheet of paper. 'How long has he been here?' Nina asked Helen.

'About five minutes.' Helen looked dubiously over at him. Finding himself the object of attention, he shuffled the papers on the desk and turned to face them. Nina saw a fixed smile creep over his lips and stay there. 'He came back to the ward and I told him there was a slight problem and he was to go and see you and Mr Farris. He stood outside the cubicle for a minute or two, then he said he had some notes to write first and he'd be with you as soon as possible.'

Nina felt a shiver go down her spine. So there *had* been someone listening to their conversation. Why hadn't he come straight into the cubicle to deal with the problem? She walked up to the nurses' station, James in step behind her, though she wasn't aware of him. 'Would you like to come into my office, Dr Brewer?' she asked calmly, returning the smile that was still stuck across his face. 'We've had a problem with Mr Angelou, and I think you'd better hear about it.' Gathering the papers from the desk, she led the way—and James followed. After all, he reasoned, he'd been the medic who had administered the morphine antidote, and if there was an inquiry he would be involved, so he might as well get properly involved now. He seated himself beside Dr Brewer who, despite looking relaxed as he slumped casually in his seat, had unusually white knuckles.

Nina took the prescription form from the Angelou file. 'One of my nurses administered an overdose of morphine sulphate to your patient,' she said simply. 'When you look at this prescription sheet you'll know why.'

He took it casually, read it and then scanned it again. 'I'm afraid I don't see anything wrong at all, Sister,' he said coolly. 'What's supposed to be wrong with it?'

'It says 40 mg of morphine sulphate. As you know, we don't normally give a dose of much more than 10 mg.' Nina clenched her fists and dug her nails into her palms under the desk. How would Sister Parker have handled this? Not by flying off the handle, that was for sure. She would be calm and collected if it killed her.

'I'm afraid I don't know what you're talking about, Sister.' Tony Brewer looked at her with a calculatedly confused gesture. 'It says 10 mg quite clearly here—I don't think there can be any ambiguity at all.'

'May I?' Nina reached out and took the paper herself. Not that she needed to read it, she knew

what it said—but she had to look as if she was being
entirely fair here. She cast her eyes over it. *Inj.
Morphine sulphate 10 mg*, it read. She looked at it
again. There was no doubt, the handwriting of the
figure was quite clear. Her throat went dry.
Perhaps it was the wrong prescription sheet? No, it
said Angelou at the top . . . Then she noticed that,
held up against the light from the window, there
was a tiny opaque blob where the original figure
had been. She held it up high, so that he could see
that she'd rumbled him. 'This is very odd.' She
turned to James, who was watching, bemused. 'Dr
Farris, you read this prescription sheet, didn't you?
And you know that it originally authorised a dose
of 40 mg of morphine. Yet now it says 10 mg very
clearly. The strangest thing of all,' she went on,
trying to sound concerned and confused, 'is that the
original figure appears to have been covered over
with Tippex and a new one written in. Look.'

James reached out for it grimly and read it. Tony
Brewer's face had gone pale. 'Look——' he began,
but James cut him short.

'Dr Brewer and I should discuss this alone,
Sister.' He gave Nina the kind of warning look that
indicated that he'd take no nonsense from her.
Anyway, Nina thought as she got up, she had the
upper hand in this situation. She had a cast-iron
witness *and* the evidence that Dr Brewer had
tampered with the prescription sheet. That must
have been what he was doing while she and James
were in the cubicle. No wonder he wanted to alter
the prescription sheet before he had to confront

them! He'd assumed that only she and her nurses had seen the sheet—he couldn't have counted on James Farris being there and seeing it for himself. And it would be easy for him just to deny the whole thing if it was only a couple of nurses who could bear witness against him. But a surgeon—that was different. Suppressing a triumphant smile, Nina left them to it. She knew what would happen. James would press Tony to come clean about it. He would admit his error and she and her staff would be exonerated.

'I think we could both do with a cup of coffee,' James remarked as she was about to close the door. 'Would you arrange it for us, Sister?'

'Of course.' Nina gave him a serene smile, and he realised with a start that she had never smiled at him like that before. And she never would again, he thought dryly when he and Tony Brewer emerged from her office twenty minutes later. Dr Brewer went straight to see Mr Angelou and, finding him not much the worse for wear, hotfooted it from the ward. James hung around the nurses' station.

'Where's Sister?' he asked Helen Osborne when she came to the desk to check the Kardex.

'She's doing a round with one of the anaesthetists.' Helen looked at him worriedly. 'Is everything going to be all right, Mr Farris? Nina's only an Acting Sister at the moment, and something like this . . .'

'Honestly, MI5 could learn a lot from the way information circulates in a hospital!' James smiled, and tried to look confident. 'I hope everything's going to be all right—if Sister keeps her head no one should come to any harm from this.'

'But I thought Dr Brewer had as good as admitted it was his fault by faking the prescription form?' Helen pointed out.

'Nothing is ever as simple as it seems,' James responded enigmatically. 'Look, I can't hang around waiting for her, I've got my own rounds to do before I spend the afternoon in Theatre. Does Sister take a lunch break?'

'Only a very quick one on operating day,' Helen replied.

He tapped his fingers impatiently on the desk. 'That's no good, we've got to have a proper talk.' He took a sheet of paper and scribbled a note on it. Helen watched, even though she pretended to be labelling some samples to go off to the path. lab. 'Give this to Sister, please,' James instructed, handing it to her. 'Though goodness knows why I try to keep things confidential—you could give her the message verbatim, couldn't you?' And with that cynical comment, which left Helen blushing, he was off.

'You mean he didn't haul Tony Brewer over the carpet and go off to report that it was *his* fault?' Nina stood speechlessly holding James's note while Helen recounted their conversation. Nina shook her head, not comprehending the situation. 'And now he's left this, asking me to meet him in the senior staff sitting-room at five, so that we can discuss the situation!' Helen didn't admit that she already knew that particular development. 'We'll see about this! He's obviously going to try to get Tony Brewer off the hook. Well, it's not going to work.'

'Nina—sorry, *Sister*,' Helen interrupted quietly, 'Mr Farris did say that we've all got to keep our heads about this.'

Nina gave her a withering look. 'He would, wouldn't he? He's going to propose a cover-up. After all, he and Dr Brewer are both men and both senior members of the medical profession. They like to stick together, and who cares if a nurse or two goes to the wall?' She poked a finger menacingly in Helen's direction. 'Well, I'm not having it!'

She would normally have finished her shift at four o'clock, but on operating days and when she had a particularly difficult workload, she was quite prepared to stay on for an extra hour or two—in fact it wasn't unknown for a conscientious Sister to come in at seven a.m. on a busy day and to stay until late in the afternoon. You had to be flexible, and it was the younger woman, and those without families, who were able to be so without the worries of children and a husband waiting at home for their dinner. Before setting off for her confrontation with Mr Farris—because she knew that it *was* going to be a confrontation and not a pleasant meeting —Nina combed her hair carefully and put on a smear of lipgloss and a touch of eyeshadow. Not that he'd notice, but it was part of her preparation for meeting the enemy. 'My warpaint,' she thought grimly as she set off up the corridor, having handed everything over to the senior staff nurse who would take over for the evening.

A thousand thoughts were buzzing in her head, not least the troublesome one of why James Farris had kissed her the other night. It kept bothering her, even though she had decided the answer that same evening as she'd walked home. He had wanted to punish her, prove that despite her quick tongue he was stronger than her. He wouldn't hit her, he was too civilised for that, so instead he had kissed her—not because he liked her but because he wanted to prove his dominance.

Despite having come to this decision and roundly condemned the man for it, Nina couldn't help but still ponder over it. Not, of course, she told herself, that she wanted to imagine that James was actually romantically interested in her. The idea was ridiculous. He'd proved all along that he didn't give a damn about her. Well, that wasn't strictly true, the voice of conscience told her. He had come to rescue her from the police station. He had given her the key to her flat. He had opened the door for her the other day. He had even put flowers in her flat. And he had been thoughtful enough to give her the other key, so that she wouldn't feel that he could prowl around up there when he liked. All in all he had been quite good about things. Very good, prompted her conscience. In fact in some ways he wasn't unlike Dr Bruce Milne, her perfect doctor. Nina chuckled to herself as she waited for the lift.

Didn't that just prove the gap between fantasy and reality? The invisible doctor was a paragon; the real thing was just about to sell her up the river.

She got to the sitting-room where senior staff, including Sisters, could meet or relax for a while between shifts. There were modern easy-chairs and a large table in an alcove, which was used for private meetings or presentations. Only a couple of weeks ago Colin Sturgis had received his wedding presents over a glass of wine. His face when he had seen the tablecloth and napkins from the Sisters had been a picture! Today there was no one here. Nina helped herself to a cup of coffee from the jug which was kept on a hotplate and topped up every hour or two by the catering staff. It tasted as if it had been standing there brewing for weeks on end. She sat down nervously on a red chair with chipped pine arms and looked at the clock. He was ten minutes late. She'd give him another five and then she'd leave. Who did he think he was, asking her to wait?

At fifteen minutes past five exactly, just as she was about to pick up her bag and leave, James came tearing in. He had obviously come straight from the theatre because he was still wearing the green drawstring trousers that are used in sterile conditions. He had dispensed with his top, and was wearing a plain white T-shirt and a crumpled white coat over the top. A stethoscope dangled dangerously from one pocket. Nina noticed, as he threw himself into the chair opposite hers, that there was a large spot of dark blood on the knee of his greens.

He looked down and saw it too. 'Oh dear—I should have changed them,' he muttered with uncharacteristic lack of confidence. Nina looked at him in agreement. Everyone knew that surgeons and doctors and nurses got spattered with gore from time to time, but that was supposed to be kept a big secret from the general public. It ruined people's confidence if, in walking round the hospital, they kept bumping into staff who looked as if they'd spent a morning in an abattoir. All bloody or dirty clothing was strictly off limits in public areas.

'What's this all about?' she demanded, with characteristic bluntness.

James looked at her and despaired. It was no good expecting pleasantries, he supposed. But it would have helped if she'd looked like an old battleaxe. Instead of which, she looked so stern and darkly glittering with indignation that he wanted to kiss her all over again. 'We've got a bit of a problem,' he started.

'No, we haven't,' Nina contradicted. 'Tony Brewer is entirely in the wrong, and he's made his position even worse by trying to cover it up. I've got you and Jane as witnesses . . .'

James's slow shake of the head stopped her in her tracks. 'I don't think I can. You see,' he shrugged, 'Tony has already had a caution this year. There was some mix-up in medication for an asthma patient a couple of months ago, he tells me, and he was put on probation, as it were. If he gets blamed for *this* mix-up too it could be the end of his career. It was a case of him mainly to blame and you partly to blame, Nina, and I don't want to see him dismissed for something that could have happened to anyone.'

Nina was pale with fury and with a vision of the future. 'Do you know what'll happen if I get blamed? They'll demote me back to staff nurse and I'll never make it to Sister!'

'Don't be ridiculous.' James had seen how worried she was. 'They may not make you Sister, but you'll soon be up there in a couple of years. And surely it's better *that* happens than that a young doctor loses his job?'

'A young doctor who keeps going round poisoning people!' blasted Nina. 'Come to think of it, I'm not sure he wasn't in trouble a year or two ago for giving someone barbiturates just before they went down to Theatre. You're going to stick up for someone like that and let *me* take the rap?' She looked at him disgustedly.

James was taken back by this news that Tony Brewer apparently made a habit of getting things wrong. He'd assumed that he'd had a run of bad luck. It could happen to anyone. In fact somewhere along the line almost every doctor and surgeon made a mistake, fatal or otherwise. Doctors were only human, after all. But it was beginning to sound as if Tony Brewer was even more human than most.

'There's something else,' Nina added. 'If I get fired or demoted I won't have enough money to pay the mortgage on your flat.' The thought had only just occurred to her, and it bothered her even more than the idea of not getting her promotion. She'd been overdramatic about never getting promoted to Sister, certainly. But the idea of having to sell the new flat even before she had had time to move into it was a terrifying one.

'I don't think there's any need to worry about that.' James tried to play the situation down. 'Surely Dr Milne will help you out? I mean, if he's going to be sharing the place with you . . .'

'It's none of your business,' snapped Nina, cursing the day that she'd invented that superman, Dr Milne. Deciding that that sounded too evasive, she said, 'Dr Milne has his own financial responsibilities. He won't be helping me out.'

'Oh.' James thought about that one for a moment. So did Nina. What did it mean? they both wondered. To James it was increasingly obvious. Dr Milne had to be a married man, with a wife and children to support and no money to spare. He must have a lot of children, James thought wistfully. A top endocrinologist was worth a great deal, even in the NHS. 'Anyway,' he said as brightly as he could, 'it probably won't happen. I think the best thing will be just to say that there was some confusion, a great deal going on on the ward, and that one of the student nurses made an error. You can even blame me if you want, and say that I insisted on calling you away at a moment when you should have been supervising your staff. You won't get into too much trouble, your student'll get off lightly, I'll be told to be a bit more careful in future and we'll be congratulated on spotting and dealing with the problem in time. Everyone emerges from it without a stain on their character, no harm done. It's the best way.'

'No, it's not, it's corrupt!' Nina leapt to her feet. 'I thought you were more decent than that, James!' Her face was distraught, and he could see that despite herself, tears were welling in her eyes. 'You don't rate me much as a nurse, or even as a person, I know, but I've never, *never* made an error on the ward before. That's why they're going to make me Sister at the age of twenty-seven. And if you get your way you'll have blotted my copybook for no reason at all.'

He got up and edged towards her. 'Nina, please —I *do* care, I don't want to see you in trouble——'

'And that's why you're going to stick up for Tony Brewer? You're a worm!' She raised her hand and went to hit him in the chest. Instead he caught it and, thrown off balance, she cannoned into him. He lurched backwards and put his arm around her to keep her upright, and Nina found herself with her head buried against his neck and her palm hard up against his chest. She could feel the outline of one firm pectoral muscle beneath her fingers, and for a moment she was aware of the strength and protectiveness of his arms. 'Let me go,' she instructed through gritted teeth, unable to understand the overwhelming desire to rest there in his arms.

James looked down on her, his blue eyes sparkling. 'I like it like this,' he said gently.

'But I don't!' Nina ground out, trying to prise herself away from him. He wasn't squeezing her, not hurting her—just holding her close, with one of his palms in the small of her back and the other higher, around her shoulders. 'Take your hands off me!'

'Have you ever seen *The Taming of the Shrew*?' asked James, amused for some reason.

'I don't want a literary discussion. I just want you to let me go,' Nina protested. The smell of him frightened her. It was so long since she'd been as close to a man, any man, as this. There was something so virile and forceful about him that it reminded her of Alan and the last time she had stood with a man like this. He had been strong and enveloping too.

'Just thought I'd warn you that eventually the shrew gets her man.' James waited for some gritty response, the kind he had come to expect from her, but it didn't come.

'Stop it! Stop it!' Her cry was from the heart. He immediately recognised her anguish and let her go. 'Leave me alone, don't touch me!' Nina backed away from him, the tears smarting in her eyes and rolling on to her cheeks. He watched as if in a daze. Where had the hardened feminist disappeared to, the woman who was so tough and angry that she always had the last word? Nina bent to find her shoulderbag, which she'd dropped, but the tears in her eyes blurred everything and she couldn't find it. 'No, go away!' she cried when James approached to help her retrieve it.

'I'm sorry, Nina.' He felt helpless. He couldn't touch her without making her hysterical, yet she couldn't go in this state. 'It was just a game.' He threw his hand to his forehead. 'No, it *wasn't* just a game. Come here, let me wipe your eyes. I won't do anything, I promise.'

'I hate you!' Her voice was low and vengeful as embarrassment and shame swept through her. She'd never, never in her life been reduced to tears by a man. Even when Alan had made his confession she had managed to keep a stiff upper lip, pretend that everything was all right. No one had known how deep it had gone. She had grieved alone, where no one could see or hear her crying. And now this bloody fool had come along and made her as stupid as he was.

'Tell me what's wrong.' James was gentle, almost pleading. 'I'd prefer you to yell at me rather than see you like this. Who's hurt you? Is it Dr Milne?'

'*You're* what's wrong! Why can't you leave me alone?' Nina's anger and humiliation acted together to dry up the tears that had so suddenly overwhelmed her. 'You're always interfering, always thinking you're helping me out and doing me a favour. Why can't you understand that I don't want anything from you?' She paused for breath. 'I wouldn't even want to buy your damn flat, except that I can't get out of the deal now we've exchanged contracts. And as for your suggestion that I help you cover up for Dr Brewer, you're joking.' She found her bag, wedged under the chair. Now she was back in command of her senses, and she was going to make James pay for what he had just witnessed. 'I'm going to make sure he's fired, and

I'm going to tell everyone that *you* suggested a cover-up. You'd prefer to put patients' lives at risk rather than see a fellow doctor in trouble, and as far as I'm concerned that stinks. And so do you,' she added for good measure. 'I suggest you have a shower before you make anyone else cry!' And with that, head held high in the air despite the fact that the tears were still damp on her cheeks, she walked out.

CHAPTER SEVEN

'THERE'S nothing like a game of squash to work out your aggression!' Angie Sinclair rubbed her hair vigorously with a towel. 'I always feel as if I could float after a good workout, don't you?'

Nina laughed, drying between her toes and pulling on her socks. 'I don't play often enough, so when I do I just feel shattered. 'Like now. And I'm going to ache terribly in the morning!'

'When are you moving?' Angie had finished with the towel and was now trying to comb her hair into shape. Nina was lucky. Hers was kept very short —she had the kind of well-shaped, pert face which suited short hair. And it had enough natural wave to it to dry naturally and still look good.

'Next Wednesday, on my day off. That's the day the sale is completed, anyway.'

'You don't sound very enthusiastic about it.' Angie raised her eyebrows.

Nina sighed. She couldn't tell anyone the truth. The hospital was full of rumours anyway, ever since the day that she'd gone to report Tony Brewer and James Farris to the SNO, and to give details about the overdose on her ward. Someone had also overheard the row in the senior staff room and seen her coming out in a state. If she were now to announce to the world that she was moving into James

Farris's house there'd be no end to it all. Nurses were among the world's worst when it came to pairing people off together—and just because most of *them* wouldn't mind marrying and becoming Mrs Farris, they assumed that she wouldn't either. 'I've got a lot on my mind,' she explained to Angie. 'There's the inquiry coming up the day after tomorrow, and if that goes against me I probably won't be able to afford the flat. Anyway, moving's such a bore. I've packed most of my stuff, and then I keep finding that I've put away things I need. And Anna's moving down to London at the weekend, so the place is getting quite miserable and deserted.'

Angie was sympathetic. 'Come and stay with us for a few nights if you'd like. We've got a spare room, and at least you wouldn't feel as if you're camping out.'

Nina shook her head. 'No, thanks. I'll see it through on my own—I'm very independent.'

'Too independent, if you ask me,' said Angie with a derisive snort. 'You know, Nina, you can have too much of a good thing. There's a difference between standing on your own two feet and being pig-headed about things. You need to know your own limitations and accept help when it's offered. Otherwise you get isolated and. ungrateful, and after a while no one offers any more.'

'Ha, ha!' Nina made light of it, but it struck an uncomfortable chord. That was what had happened with James. He had found her struggling upstairs with a cane chair the other evening—the damned thing had got jammed—and all he'd said was, 'Don't scratch the banisters if you can help it,' and disappeared into his own flat. There was a time when he would have offered her a hand. Now he just left her to get on with it—which was fine by her, she insisted.

'I could do with a drink. Come and have one with me,' insisted Angie, packing her sports gear into her bag.

'It's years since I spent an evening in the bar here,' Nina protested. 'I don't honestly think I want to spend the time with a horde of junior doctors and student nurses.'

'You're out of touch. Quite a few of the older staff come here now that the squash and tennis courts have been built. They've done up the bar too, and there's a place where you can get snacks. It's good, you know—and cheaper than a pub.'

'All right, I'll give it a try,' Nina conceded dubiously. And Angie was right. Instead of the old place, with its red plastic seating and stained formica tables, there was a new brick and pine edifice, with plush blue chairs, a subtly-lit bar packed with gleaming glasses and lots of discreet alcoves where, Nina imagined, numerous liaisons were kept. Pictures of the hospital and moorland landscapes dotted the walls, and there were even some colourful splodges from the children's ward. 'That's my doing,' Angie boasted. 'They were so good that I had them framed. Then I didn't know what to do with them, until I noticed that space on the wall. I asked if they wanted to put something up there, and when they said yes I brought my kids' stuff along. They were a bit shocked at first, but they brighten the place up.'

'They certainly do,' Nina agreed. It was in fact a very nice place—and because so many of the faces were familiar, it felt like coming into a club rather than walking into a strange pub. She was inspecting the room more closely, counting the number of arched alcoves that had been built into the wall and wondering where the wide archway led to, when her sweeping gaze caught a pair of eyes, swept past and then returned.

Who was it? She peered through the gloom, then suddenly found she was staring straight into the eyes of James Farris. With a start she swivelled on her chair and faced the opposite direction. It was a great pity that it was just a boring blank brick wall. 'What's wrong?' asked Angie, making her own circuit of the area. 'Ah, the famous Farris!'

'Spare me, please, Angie. Despite what the bush telegraph in the nurses' canteen would have, I assure you that we can't stand the sight of each other.'

'That's the first sign,' said Angie with mock gravity. 'When I first met Tim I hated him. He was so arrogant, and he kept trying to do things for me—so kind and considerate it made me want to hit him! Then after a little while he decided not to waste his time on me and went off with someone more willing—at which point I realised that I'd rather liked having him around. Fortunately he realised he'd made a great mistake,' she joked, 'and didn't play too hard to get.' She peered again through the half-light. 'Which may be the case with this particular relationship. Don't look now, Nina——'

'I'm not going to look at all,' Nina protested flatly.

'But he's with . . .' Angie strained her eyes. 'Ah, yes, she's hiding behind him! It's that one who thinks she looks like Marilyn Monroe—you know, the new girl from Neuro. The one with the platinum blonde hair and the wiggle in her walk. Come on,' she said in disgust, 'there aren't *that* many nurses who've tried to get away with fishnet tights on the ward.'

'Typical.' Nina took a gulp of her spritzer and refused to be goaded into turning round and taking a look at this epitome of slavish womanhood. 'Just the kind of girl he'd go for—some eager-to-please sex object.'

Angie looked at her knowingly. 'Seriously, you'd better not turn round. Tony Brewer's just come in with a couple of his friends, and we don't want a fight.'

'What do you mean by that?' Nina glanced at her worriedly.

Angie leaned across the table and patted her on the arm. 'It's an open secret that Tony Brewer's not the most reliable doctor in the hospital. He's made more mistakes in four years than any other doctor would make in a lifetime, and everyone knows that. But he's popular, particularly with some of the other young doctors, and the student nurses.'

Nina frowned. 'This is unbelievably hypocritical!

Everyone knows he's incompetent, yet because he swaggers around drinking too much no one wants him to get into trouble for it. Which camp are you in, Angie?'

Angie seemed surprised at the ferocity of the question. 'Yours! I can't stand him. He deigns to come up on a medical emergency and nine times out of ten I have to point out all the symptoms and contra-indications to him. And he always reeks of booze. There's no one in a senior position who'll defend him—all I meant was that you're not going to be flavour of the month with some of the junior staff.'

'It doesn't bother me one bit,' Nina said dryly. It was odd, but suddenly all the pleasure had gone out of her evening. Knowing that Tony Brewer was sitting there, able to throw imaginary darts at her back, made her feel uncomfortable. 'Look,' she apologised, finishing her drink, 'I'm tired after that game of squash, so I think I'll go home now—if you don't mind?'

'No.' Angie smiled. 'Let me finish my drink and I'll come with you. Tim'll be home by now, and I might as well see what I can of him.'

It was dark outside. Nina walked with Angie to the car park. 'Hop in and I'll drive you home,' offered Angie, but Nina refused.

'It's in the opposite direction to the way you're going. Anyway, I fancy a walk.' She waved good-bye to the tail-lights of Angie's Metro, then turned back through the car park to where a broad, well-lit footpath ran behind the club to the hospital. It was a pleasant evening, with a light breeze, and she was striding along thinking of the move and, more particularly, the coming inquiry into the Mr Angelou affair. As she rounded a bend in the path and found herself in a pool of blackness, where one of the lamps had burned out, the sound of running footsteps reached her—and in a couple of seconds a figure came tearing up to her.

'Stop a minute!' It was Tony Brewer. Nina kept on walking. 'I thought I told you to slow down!' he called angrily, matching her stride for stride. 'I want to have a word with you.'

'I don't have anything to say to you,' stated Nina, walking as fast as she could. She wasn't going to break into a trot or let him know that she was bothered by him—but she could smell the alcohol on his breath, and his tone was far from friendly.

'Oh yes, you do.' He wheeled round in front of her, blocking the path. She immediately turned and walked back the way they'd both come, trying not to get alarmed. She clenched her fists and prepared herself in the way she had been taught at her self-defence class. Tony swore loudly at her and, coming up behind her, knocked her into the haw-thorn hedge that butted on to the tennis courts. The prickles pierced her red cotton sweater, but when she tried to pull herself free of them he blocked her way. 'Right,' he said, triumphant at having caught her, 'you just tell me what you're going to say on Thursday. I want to know what lies you're going to tell them about me.'

'I'm not going to tell them any lies,' Nina

snapped back, wrenching herself out of the hedge defiantly and side-stepping him. 'I'm going to tell them the truth—and I shall also tell them that you tried to intimidate me tonight.'

'You bitch!' A string of other, more foul, names sprang from his lips. 'You Women's Libbers, you're all the same—there's nothing you like more than destroying men, is there? Not that you're a proper woman in the first place,' he taunted, loping round her so that she had to step backwards, sideways, forwards, but never making any progress. Fear began to creep over her. If no one came, he could keep this up indefinitely. She tried to spin round and run away from him, but he was faster than her and within less than a couple of seconds had caught up with her and grabbed her by the scruff of the neck. 'Look,' he said with drunken lack of logic, 'I'm prepared to be reasonable. If you just tell them on Thursday that it was your fault I'll forget all about this.' Nina stared hard at him, stubbornly silent. If it had been anyone else, anyone she had known wouldn't hurt her, she would have argued and fought like a demon. The difference in this situation was that she felt absolutely sure that Tony Brewer would do her harm if she rounded on him. He had been drinking very heavily, and he was a worried man. In this situation you couldn't rely on him, even if he was a doctor, not to do something stupid.

He swore at her again. '*You* don't even have to get into trouble for it—you can blame it on your student nurse, and she'll just be reprimanded and put back a term. Come on, it's the only sensible thing to do. Isn't it?' He looked menacingly at her.

'You're an even nastier piece of work than I'd imagined,' Nina said, coldly, mustering all the calm she could. Her heart was pounding in her ears. The sensible thing to do would be to go along with him, say yes, say that the last thing she wanted to do was cause trouble for him—but she'd be damned if she was going to let him bully her.

He shook her as if she was a naughty child, and she felt her teeth rattle in her head. 'You're a stupid little cow!' he yelled. 'No wonder you haven't got a man. No one in their right mind would go anywhere near you!' Nina lashed out at him, but only succeeded in punching him on the arm. Self-defence classes were all very well if muggers and attackers approached you from the right direction and held you in a copybook grip, but no one had taught her what to do when someone was hauling her around by the neck of her sweater and pushing her about like a puppet. Tony changed his hold on her and she felt the neckband of her jumper cut into her throat, bringing tears to her eyes. He'd throttle her if he wasn't careful! She tried to yell and all that came out was a gargling rasp. Frantically she scrabbled at her throat, trying to free herself and get some air, but it was in vain. She kicked out blindly, panic-stricken now—and from out of the blue there came a strange whumping noise and the grip on her was suddenly released. She fell to the ground, her hands around her throat, catching her breath in great gasps.

'I don't think I've ever known anyone to get themselves involved in as many dramatic situations as you.' A tall figure bent over her. Then his voice changed. 'Good grief, you're covered in blood! Nina, say something—are you all right?' James dropped to his knees by her side and gathered her in his arms. She was so momentarily shell-shocked that she allowed him to examine the long scratch on her temple, where one of the thorns from the hedge had drawn a surprising amount of blood. She had also scraped a wide strip of skin clean off the back of her hand somehow, and the blood from that was over her chin and neck, where she had tried to pull herself free. His fingers gently touching the red friction burn round her throat roused her from her state of relieved shock.

'Get off!' she ordered ungraciously, suddenly realising that she was sitting half-prone across his knees. The back of her head was resting against his shoulder, and he was balancing her as gently as if she'd been a week-old baby. She sat up, slid off his lap and began stiffly to get to her feet. Tony Brewer was struggling upright too. He looked at her, did a double-take and muttered,

'Oh, my God!' He turned helplessly to James. 'I didn't mean to . . .' He raised both hands to his head and buried his face, as if he was emerging from a nightmare. 'I had no idea! I didn't hit her—she'll tell you I didn't hit her!'

Nina, not realising that her face and hands were smeared with blood as if she'd been in a bad car crash, didn't understand this sudden reaction.

James did, though. His eyes, normally so blue and friendly, glittered with anger. 'I wish I had the time to teach you a lesson or two,' he snarled. 'You're lucky, though. I've got to take Nina into A&E so we can find out what damage you've done.'

'No, you're not!' The victim of the attack stoically picked up her sports bag.

'You'll do as you're told.' James rounded on her with a glare. Whether it was delayed reaction to what had happened or just the pain of her hand, which suddenly hit her, she didn't know, but for once she was silent. 'Can you walk?' asked James, offering her his arm.

She didn't deign to reply, but instead paced in front of him, down the last fifty yards of the path, which opened on to the staff car park behind the hospital. To tell the truth, her legs *did* feel a bit wobbly, she thought as she descended the three steps. For some reason the ground kept coming up to meet her foot and then sinking away when she went to move. She gulped and reached out for something to grab on to as her knees gave away on the last step down. There *was* something there, something warm and firm, a pair of arms that wrapped round her and lifted her off the ground . . . 'You idiot!' she heard him say. 'Oh, Nina, what am I going to do about you?' And she could have sworn, though she wasn't quite herself at the time, that he kissed her softly on the cheek.

The next thing she knew, she was laid out on a couch in Accident and Emergency. James and a student nurse were fussing round her, the student cleaning up the wound on her hand while James dabbed at her face with a wet swab. 'Hello again,' he said dryly as she opened her eyes. 'Thought you said you could walk without help?' He winked infuriatingly at her. 'Close your left eye—I'm going to put a steri-strip over that little gash on your temple.' Without thinking, Nina closed her right eye. James looked despairingly at the nurse, who was watching them, obviously amused by what she saw. 'Is she concussed or just stupid?' he asked her. '*Left* eye, dear.' Nina gritted her teeth and shut the correct eye. She felt his fingers, cool and smooth, applying the adhesive tape which would hold the sides of the scratch together and help it heal cleanly. A plaster would do just as well, she thought privately. He was making a mountain out of a molehill. The nurse picked a bit of grit out of the back of her hand and she let out an ouch.

'Don't fuss,' said James unsympathetically. 'You get yourself into these scrapes, and you should be prepared to take the consequences.'

Nina shot a disgusted look at him, a look that turned even more venomous when he produced an A&E treatment form. 'Name?' he enquired solicitously.

'You know it,' she rasped. If only she'd had something to throw at him and now witnesses to watch his humiliation!

'Not your middle name.' He waited, pen poised. 'Then there's the little matter of your age, your address and how you came to have this accident.'

'Catherine. Twenty-seven. Blackwater Court,' she rapped out. 'And I tripped over and fell into a bush.'

The nurse looked at her very strangely. 'That's a matter of opinion,' said James, filling the form in rapidly. 'I've never met a bush who'd half-strangled its victim before. Injuries and treatment. Hmm.' He gave her a peculiar smile. 'Injuries mostly to your pride, I suppose. Everything else is very superficial.' Nina's throbbing hand didn't feel at all superficial. Nor did the tight sensation in her throat. 'Treatment—antiseptic, dressings and sympathy.'

'I haven't had the sympathy yet,' she muttered under her breath. 'You'd better not give me the whole dose at once, it might finish me off.'

He sat on the edge of the couch, a wooden speculum and a throat light in his hands. 'That's the problem, isn't it? We'll have to cancel the sympathy. You're allergic to it—at least, that's the impression I've had every time I've tried to be nice to you. Open wide.' Before she could think of something cutting he thrust his lolly-stick down her throat and was peering about. She obediently said 'Aaaah' when instructed, aware all the while of the student nurse's fascinated gaze as she put Melolin and then a bandage over the scraped hand. James was pushed up close against her. She could feel his breath on her cheek as he inspected for damage. He needed a shave, she thought disparagingly. His hair was nice and clean, though. He put down the speculum and the torch and ran his hands lightly over her throat and up under her ears. 'Does it hurt?' She shook her head.

'Not much. It's just a bit tender.'

'Your larynx is a bit red and there's some swelling, so you'll probably find it a bit difficult to swallow—but no lasting damage. Stick to fluids for forty-eight hours and you should be all right.' He shifted on the bed to see what the student nurse had been doing. The hand was neatly bound up and she was just piling all the bits on to the trolley. He handed her the used tongue depressor and an unopened pack of steri-strips. 'Thanks, Nurse. You go back to what you were doing—I'll see Sister Newington home.'

'I'll call a cab,' Nina insisted, swinging her legs down.

'I'm in charge this evening, and you'll do what I tell you.' James was suddenly stern again. 'You could have brained yourself if you'd fallen down those steps.' Nina hesitated. To be honest, she didn't think she had the strength to argue. Her knees still felt as if they'd been put on back to front and her head as if she'd taken some kind of sleeping pill. She waited while he scrubbed his hands again at the sink by the side of the couch. She even waited while he picked up the bag containing her sports gear. And when he held out his arm to her she unwillingly put her own through it. If she passed out again it would only give him another excuse to patronise her. Better to get the whole humiliating thing over as quickly as possible.

Strangely, she didn't want to talk about what had

happened. It was too soon after the event to discuss it. She wanted just to block it out for a few hours, not to go over and over every detail. James led her out to the car park and to a dark-coloured Golf. He said nothing, for which she was grateful. She noticed the way he opened the passenger door for her and put her inside before he went round to open his own door, and was thankful that he hadn't left her standing there on her own while he got in. They drove in silence through the streets, passing the bright neon sign of the Regal Cinema, still with its porn pics on display. On any other night Nina wouldn't have been able to resist a cheap jibe —asking him if he'd seen the latest offering—but tonight she didn't have the energy for any of that. There was just enough spark left in her to make her feel peeved with herself that she could so easily be brought to her knees like this, and a rumble of indignation that it had been *him* who had come along and saved her. But she was pleased that he had. She tried not to think about what might have happened if no one had come to her rescue.

'Down here?' James pointed down a side street.

'No, the next one.' Even her voice sounded feeble and throaty. They pulled up outside the modern development where she and Anna had a flat. Nina fumbled for the door handle. 'Thanks.' She kept her eyes well down; she wasn't going to fawn all over him.

'I'll come up with you. Is your friend in?' He was out of his seat and round to her side of the car before she could gather the energy to object.

'I'm sure she is—there's really no need for you to come in,' Nina tried to protest. But she didn't really mean it, and anyway, James didn't take the slightest bit of notice. He helped her climb the stairs, one hand lightly holding her elbow, the other in the small of her back. They stopped at the bend at the top. 'I don't know what's wrong with me,' she tried to joke. 'I feel as if I'm made of blancmange!' James said nothing. What he would really liked to have done, of course, was to pick her up and carry her—not to her own home, but to his, where he could have kept a proper eye on her. But he knew instinctively that she would have hated being carted around like that, like a piece of luggage without a mind of her own. And he didn't want to distress her any more this evening. She couldn't see herself; she had no idea of how white her face was and how shaky her hand felt. He smiled wryly as she struggled to get her key in the front door of the flat. There were a lot of women who would love to be picked up and carried away and treated like children; he admired Nina's independence. He respected her for it, even though he had suffered through it in the past.

Nina couldn't get the key in the lock, no matter how hard she tried. There just didn't seem to be any strength in her muscles. Why didn't he take it from her and open it, instead of making her look like a fool? 'Will you do it?' she asked sharply at last. 'Otherwise it'll be dawn before we get in.' James smiled to himself, and she caught an infuriating glimpse of his grin. Despite herself, she couldn't help smiling too. Poor man! He couldn't do anything right, and it looked as if he had begun to accept the fact with good grace.

There were no lights on inside. 'I'll stay with you until your friend gets back,' said James in the kind of calm but firm voice which Nina didn't have the strength to disobey.

'There's no need,' she began, but he cut her short.

'You're right, there *is* no need. But I'd feel happier if I knew there was someone here tonight —and that's all there is to it,' he finished, opening doors and familiarising himself with the layout. 'Do you want a bath before you go to bed?'

'You sound like my mother.' She stood swaying before him with an amused light in her eyes.

'I pity the poor woman,' James said grimly, taking her by the arm and leading her to one of the bedrooms. 'Yours?' She shook her head. He opened the walk-in cupboard door, which made her laugh, before he found her room. 'Have you got a hot water bottle?' Again she shook her head.

'I packed it. It's at Arcadia Gardens.'

Leaving her sitting on the bed, he went to fetch the convector heater from the sitting-room. 'You're cold,' he explained, plugging it in. 'I'll go and make you something to drink. You get into bed.' And with that he went off and left her. Nina couldn't help feeling like a child, and wishing she had the strength to rebel and push him out. Then she began to realise just how ropey she felt—and despite everything she felt a tinge of relief that he was here.

James bashed around in the kitchen, torn between feeling uncomfortable, because he knew she hated this kind of fuss, and his conviction as a doctor that she shouldn't be left alone. He'd just make sure she was all right with as little fuss and as much professional efficiency as possible, he decided. There was no milk in the fridge—in fact the whole place looked as if it was in the process of being packed up. He couldn't see a saucepan anywhere. In disgust he rooted out some elderly lemons and a bottle of Scotch that had been hidden behind the bread bin.

'Can I come in?' He knocked and waited for a reply, but there was none, so he cautiously entered her bedroom. She had slipped into bed, he was pleased to see. Her clothes lay in a heap on the floor and he guessed from the way that she held the duvet tightly up around her neck that she wasn't wearing a nightdress. The thought stirred him, but he tried not to appear too interested in her bare shoulders. 'Have a sip of this.' He handed her one glass and took a mouthful of his own, not just to convince her that it wasn't poison but also because he felt that his own spirits could do with some help.

She tasted it gingerly. 'It's just lemon and honey and a slug of Scotch. It'll warm you up and make your throat feel better.'

Nina gave him a disbelieving look. 'You can't fool me. I've heard about men like you, who get girls into bed and lull them into a false sense of security with vast quantities of Scotch.'

James grinned and knelt by the side of the bed. 'You're safe with me, kid,' he said in his best Humphrey Bogart voice. Nina took another swig of the concoction, finished it and handed him the empty glass. As she reached out with it he caught a glimpse of her bare breast exposed as the duvet fell forwards. He wished he hadn't. It wasn't right to feel this way about a patient. Maybe he *should* take his chance, kiss her and caress her now while she was still shocked and almost dead on her feet. She was feeling vulnerable; now of all times she would accept him. He was tempted. Once she was back to her normal self again he'd never stand a chance. But it was only a stupid passing thought, and he felt disgusted with himself for even contemplating it.

Nina turned over in bed, her back to him. She knew it wasn't right, she knew she shouldn't go to sleep with him there. She knew she should tell him to go, tell him to stop treating her like some helpless child . . . But she didn't have any control over herself any more. It was as if her mind and body were slowly shutting down, bit by bit. First her knees. Then her voice. Now her eyes were closing of their own accord.

She was asleep. James carefully eased the duvet up around her shoulders and tucked it in. Then, on impulse, he released it again, softly kissed the nape of her neck, and covered her over. He stood up, looking at the bare walls, the omnipresent cardboard box with its bitty collection of stationery, woolly gloves, tatty paperbacks. It was pathetic really. He needed someone to love, and of all the girls in all the hospitals in all the world he'd had to choose her—the only one who was convinced she didn't need him. He felt so helpless. Tonight had been a breakthrough; they'd managed to go a whole hour without an argument. But at what a price? He thought of Tony Brewer and decided that he'd kill him, slowly. Sitting on the end of the bed, with the bedside lamp on the floor so that Nina wouldn't be disturbed by the brightness, he planned a dozen completely unethical but extremely imaginative ways of bringing Dr Brewer to an uncomfortable end.

CHAPTER EIGHT

NINA sat nervously on her chair outside the SNO's office. From within she could hear a low murmur of voices, but they were too distant to distinguish, let alone hear what was being said. She'd been asked to arrive at ten, so that the inquiry, which the SNO's assistant said shouldn't take long, would be finished by lunchtime.

How she hated this kind of hiccup to her routine! She kicked her feet on the floor and cursed Tony Brewer for getting them all into this mess in the first place. She'd had to have the day off sick yesterday, something she'd never done before. And it didn't look good on the day before an inquiry into an error on her ward. She felt fine now. Her throat was a bit tender and her hand was still bandaged, but the scene of the night before last was really just a dim memory—a memory that made her wince to think of it. The humiliation! At the time she had felt so peculiar that she hadn't objected to James Farris barnstorming in like some super-hero and taking the whole thing over. And what was even worse, Anna had thought he was wonderful.

'I won't hear a word against him,' she had insisted, bringing Nina breakfast in bed the morning after the accident. 'He's lovely, Nina— and you know me, I'm not over the top about men in general. He seemed so thoughtful and kind . . .'

'Oh yes, *seemed*!' Nina had rasped, dripping tea on to the duvet. 'He seems all right until you get to know him, and then you realise you've been conned. He's a sexist, a chauvinist, he goes to see dirty films——'

'Yes, he told me about that,' Anna said with a twinkle in her eye. 'I can't help feeling you're a bit over the top. He explained how you'd met, and about the Regal incident. If he *was* as awful as you say he is I don't think he would have told me.' Nina cast her a look of scathing disbelief. 'He's up-front,' Anna continued. She had been *very* impressed with him last night. 'I think he's one of those naturally honest men who can't lie and can't pretend very well.'

'And he's got a beautiful blonde girlfriend,' Nina chipped in. 'I've seen her photo. So if he's as straight and true and perfect as you say there's no point in me getting friendly, is there?' She suddenly realised that she wasn't wearing the big T-shirt which she normally used in bed. Her eyes caught the pile of clothes on the floor, and the T-shirt on top, and an expression of extreme consternation crossed her features. Had *he* undressed her? She didn't think so. Surely she wasn't so far gone that she would have allowed him to do that?

'Well, he says you're to stay in bed today. He was going to call in for you and explain what had happened. And he said that if you give me any problems I'm to send for him and he'll deal with you.'

Nina gave her a withering smile. 'There, you see what a lovely person he is?'

'If you don't like him and he doesn't like you, why all this fuss? There are plenty of men *I* don't like and I just don't talk about them. But you're always harping on about the wrongs he's done you. There are some people,' Anna added with a calculating glance,' who'd say that there's no smoke without fire.'

'There are *some* people who think Tony Brewer's a saint and Terry Wogan's a sex symbol,' Nina responded. 'But they're not taken seriously.'

Anna had had to go off to work then, and Nina had knocked around in the flat on her own all day. Someone had rung the bell once, but she didn't answer it in case it turned out to be James doing his round or some other interested third party from the hospital. The phone had rung a couple of times, but she had ignored that too. And now here she was, waiting for her fate to be decided. She swallowed the little lump of worry that rose in her throat. Tony Brewer was in the wrong; his action the other night had only served to prove that. He couldn't be allowed to get away with it.

The door opened and the man in question emerged. He was wearing a very sober grey suit and looked ten years older than he had the other night, when he'd played cat and mouse with her on that dark footpath. 'Hallo.' He nodded to her and with a start she realised that he had a black eye and a piece of flesh-coloured sticking plaster across his nose. 'Look, I want to apologise for the other evening. I'd had too much to drink, and that and the worry made me loose my temper with you. I can't think what made me do it.'

Nina just stared coldly at him. 'Isn't that typical?' she murmured, with a sugary smile that melted to acid. 'You might have killed me—but it's some relief to know you'd have been sorry afterwards.'

'I don't know why I bothered.' Tony was peering nastily at her out of his one good eye. 'You're everything I said you were, Sister Newington . . .'

'Would you like to come in now?' The SNO's assistant opened the door and summoned Nina, who issued Tony Brewer her most withering glare and disappeared into the lion's den. The SNO sat at the top of the table with a representative from the Sisters' committee, an administrator whom Nina didn't recognise and, nearest her, James. He turned to look at her as she was ushered to her seat, and she saw with amazement that he had a black eye too.

'Thank you for coming, Sister,' the SNO started. 'I have some news which may come as something of a surprise for you, and that is that Dr Brewer has just offered us his resignation. Naturally I as a member of the nursing staff can't accept it, but he is on his way now to repeat the procedure with the medical authorities. This does rather put a new light on the incident we're here to investigate.'

Nina tried not to look too pleased. When she was asked to give her version of the events she did so clearly and concisely, pointing out that in falsifying the prescription sheet Dr Brewer had as good as admitted guilt. 'Yes, he's already told us about that,' the SNO nodded, seeming not to be very interested. 'I must say that I'm not entirely happy that you allowed yourself to be distracted when your student nurse was administering such an important drug——'

'That's *my* fault,' James butted in. 'Naturally I had no idea what was going on and I demanded Sister's attention. I was in a hurry.' He looked very humble, Nina thought—and this was the man who Anna said couldn't tell a lie! 'I think sometimes we doctors forget how responsible and difficult a nurse's job can be. We like to think that we're all that matters.'

The SNO looked at him dubiously, as if she'd rumbled him, but the other Sister preened slightly, as if he had just confirmed what she had known all along. 'I understand, too, that your student nurse, Jane Burns, was the first to realise the error?'

'That's right,' said Nina. 'She's extremely bright and normally my most dependable student. I can't think of a more unfortunate person to get involved with something like this. I'll be giving her a very good report when she leaves the ward.'

The SNO looked down her page of notes. 'In view of the fact that the incident was spotted so quickly and so promptly dealt with, and also taking into account that it seems that Dr Brewer's contribution to the error was the major one—and also in view of Mr Farris's selfless confession,' she added, peering disbelievingly over her spectacles, 'I think we'll leave the whole thing here. There will be a note of it on your file, Sister Newington, and also on Student Nurse Burns's, but I don't consider that anything in the case merits an official warning or disciplinary action. Of course, if it should happen again . . .'

'It won't,' said Nina firmly. 'It wouldn't have done in the first place, except for Dr Brewer.'

'Quite.' The SNO wrote something on each of the files she held in front of her, then looked up with something that might have been the shadow of a smile on her lips. 'I won't embarrass you by enquiring how all three of you came by your injuries.'

James got up to leave, and Nina spotted just the hint of a rueful grin around his mouth as he slipped past her. She went to get up herself, but was called back. 'Just a couple more things I feel I should say to you, Sister Newington,' the SNO said with a stony straight face. They waited until James had shut the door firmly behind him. 'First of all, I wanted to assure you that we're not unaware of some of the complexities of this incident.' She waved the A&E form, with Nina's name and James's signature at the bottom. 'Not that I think we'll ever get the full details.' She raised her eyebrow questioningly, but Nina said nothing. 'In a way this has been very useful for us. Dr Brewer has had an erratic career at this hospital and it may be that he'll find himself more suited to another area of practice.' Nina admired the way that people in positions of power used language. No one would ever say, 'Thank goodness, Tony Brewer's going to have to resign now,' but that was pretty much what was meant, she felt sure.

'Finally, I think you should take a week's leave from today. Your usefulness on the ward is going to be restricted while your hand heals and you've not had a break for nearly four months now. I'm also pleased to be able to tell you that when you come back you will resume your present position as a full Sister.' Nina's face must have shown her delight, for the SNO held up her hands to stop her saying anything. 'We would, however, like you to bear in mind how easily the accident with Mr Angelou occurred, Sister Newington. If you could slow down your pace and try to avoid all the madcap schemes you seem to get involved with, all of us would feel happier.'

'Of course. Thank you very much.' Nina tried to look cool, as if the idea that she would lose her promotion had never occurred to her.

At last the SNO's frost melted. She and the Sister stood up and came over to shake hands. 'This is strictly off the books,' she murmured with a discreet smile, 'but I notice that that awful cinema down the road is going to show another series of films about nurses. Do you and Sister Sinclair intend to do anything about it?'

Nina looked from one to the other. 'But I thought that madcap schemes were off limits?'

'We're quite capable of turning a blind eye to things,' the Sister said quietly. 'You could have been hauled over the coals for your last escapade there, but to be honest some of us think that it was rather courageous of you and Sister Sinclair to take a stand. Naturally this won't be heard outside these walls.' Nina could have sworn that she winked.

'Believe it or not,' the SNO murmured, steering her towards the door, 'there *are* one or two people over the age of forty in this hospital who share quite a few of your views. Congratulations, Sister.'

And with that, Nina found herself outside in the waiting room again, scarcely able to believe what her ears and brain were telling her. With an infuriating little smile pinned to her face, and saying hallo with inane cheerfulness to everyone she met en route, she made her way to the ward, just to check that everything was running smoothly and to update Jand and Helen on what had happened. Fortunately it was quiet and they were able to snatch ten minutes for a cup of coffee and share the good news. 'I'll just do an hour's paperwork before I go,' Nina insisted.

'We've got a relief Sister coming on at lunch,' Helen protested. 'You should leave it to her.'

'I'd like to have everything neat and tidy for her,' said Nina firmly, and so instead of going straight home she worked until lunchtime, making sure that everything was up-to-date. She didn't want another Sister coming on to the ward and complaining. At one o'clock she collected all her personal belongings and waved goodbye. A whole week off work! It couldn't have been better timed.

'Nina!' She was just about to leave the hospital

by the side entrance near the canteen when James's voice called her back. She didn't want to go—she didn't want to talk to him, but she knew she must. She couldn't be *so* ungrateful. 'Well?' he stood grinning in front of her. 'Didn't I say everything would be all right?'

'What do you mean by that?' she asked, taken aback by his tone.

He shrugged. 'Once I'd told them that you'd been injured and owned up that it was partly my fault that you'd got the dose wrong . . .'

'Got the dose wrong?' All her charitable thoughts began to disappear. '*I* didn't get the dose wrong, remember. And as for that ever-so-humble performance in there, they didn't believe a word of it. Ooh!' she exclaimed, 'you've got a nerve! I've been exonerated for the Angelou incident and I've been made a full Sister, and here you are trying to claim the credit for it! Will you *never* stop interfering? I'm quite capable of handling these things on my own, thank you.'

'That's not what I meant. I simply mean that you should never have worried about it in the first place. And at least you'll have some time off to move into the flat now,' he finished.

'Don't tell me you arranged that too?' Nina's eyes blazed with fury. Was there anything as infuriating as coming out of sticky situation with all flags flying, only to find that someone else had been secretly engineering things behind your back?

'They asked if you were badly hurt and I said it might be wise for you to take some time off—

particularly as you won't be able to touch the patients while you've got your hand done up like that.' James pointed to her bandage. While her hand was bound up like that she couldn't wash it properly. It was also a well-known fact that bandages and dressings could harbour germs and, on a surgical ward in particular, that could be dangerous. A nurse with a cut or scrape was excused all contact with wounds and dressings until it was healed and she could ensure that her hands were absolutely clean.

'I can't believe it!' Nina shook her head in disgust. 'Will you stop running my life for me? Before you came along I was quite capable of looking after myself——'

'You mean you haven't made a habit of getting yourself into scrapes and fights?' James looked at her disbelievingly. 'I've know you how long? I've been here a couple of months. And in that time you've been arrested, made several spectacles of yourself and almost been murdered. Honestly, Nina, you need a minder!'

Her mouth opened in indignation, but nothing emerged for a second and she just gaped at him. 'Look at you! You look as if you'd gone ten rounds with Frank Bruno. And you have the nerve to lecture me . . .'

'Excuse me.' A blushing medical student squeezed past them and out of the side door.

'In here,' muttered James, and dragged her a few feet back up the corridor and into an empty broom cupboard. It was very dim, with just a tiny skylight picking out the dusty shelves. Giant bottles of the hospital's antiseptic sat around, giving off their characteristic pong. 'You,' he told Nina with feeling, blocking off her escape from the door, 'are the most ungrateful woman I've ever met. Have you seen Tony Brewer today?'

'Yes,' said Nina, studying the skylight. It was funny, if she'd been locked in here with Tony Brewer she'd have been scared stiff. But it was only James, and he wasn't going to hurt her. She realised with surprise that she felt quite at home with him. She trusted him, though heaven knew why.

'And did you notice that he'd been in a fight?'

'Yes.' Wasn't it strange that no matter how furious James pretended to be, he couldn't rattle her? He was a big softy.

'That's because he'd been in a fight with me. Are you listening?' He brought her chin down with his fingers and made her look at him. Suddenly his voice was soft and serious. 'I've never, ever, been in a fight before. I didn't fight at school and I've never in my life hit anyone. And yet I had a stand-up fight with Tony Brewer. Can you even begin to understand what this means?'

Nina thought for a minute, cocking her head to one side. 'Well,' she deliberated, 'as he looked as if he'd come out of it worse than you, I'd say it means that you've got natural talent when it comes to brawling.'

'Give me strength!' He raised his hands to the ceiling. 'I'm absolutely crazy—I must be! No man in his right mind could love you. You're not only the most infuriating, most ungrateful, most bloody-minded woman in the world . . .'

'Please go on,' urged Nina. 'This is music to my ears, because coming from a man it's a great compliment.'

James glowered. 'Right, let's see how you like this. You're the most attractive woman I've seen for ages. I love your independence. When you're looking at me like that all I want to do is kiss you. I adore the way you throw yourself into everything you do. I think you're brave . . .'

Nina swallowed. 'That's quite enough, thank you. I'd like to go now.'

'You've got a lovely pair of legs,' James went on relentlessly, his brain rattling through all the things he knew about her, things she wouldn't want mentioned. 'I love the back of your neck, where you hair comes down in a little point. I haven't seen much of the rest of you, but I'm sure that's sexy too.'

'Stop it!' That now familiar anguished tone was back in her voice.

'Why?' He took her by the shoulders, forcing her to look at him squarely. 'Tell me *why*, Nina? Why is it that you can take every insult I throw at you, and yet when I say or do something nice you panic and freeze? What's wrong? You've got to tell me.'

'Because I hate you.'

'No, you don't. You don't even hate Tony Brewer. Hate's a destructive thing, and the only thing you're destroying is yourself. Perhaps that's it? Why do you hate yourself so much? Why do you persist in torturing yourself? Look at me.' His voice was almost pleading. 'I could make you happy, I really could. I think I love you, but you won't let me prove it.'

'You'd better forget it,' Nina sniffed, her thoughts and feelings jumbled like knotted string in the pit of her stomach. 'I don't love you, and I couldn't make you happy. And anyway, what about that blonde you've got on your mantelpiece? She looks just your type. She's the kind who wouldn't mind being bossed around.'

James looked as if he'd been slapped round the face. 'She *was* my type—or I thought she was. We nearly got married, but she called it off with only a few days to go and married my best friend instead. There, is that what you wanted to hear?' He'd gone quite pale.

'I'm sorry. I didn't know.' Nina looked down at her feet. She could understand how he felt. She thought of Alan and the humiliation she would feel if she ever had to tell anyone about him.

'You never asked,' snapped James. 'You just jumped to conclusions, as you do all the time. Abby got away without much of a fight. If I'd stood up for her more she might not have run away from me. And that's what this black eye means, Nina. I'm serious about this—I've actually thumped Tony Brewer because of you!' And then he kissed her, so gently that she barely felt his lips on her neck, tracing the red burn line round her throat and up to her ears. She tried to steel herself just to stand there and let him kiss her like a lump of dead flesh, but she couldn't. Her hand brushed up through his hair, and she realised that it was the first time she had voluntarily touched him. He knew it too, and traced a path to her lips, where he kissed her again with such tenderness that her heart nearly wept.

'That wasn't so bad, was it?' he breathed, smiling at her.

Nina felt her blood boil. One measly little kiss and he thought he'd done it—he thought that she'd just fall into his arms! She smiled secretly and kissed him in return. Encouraged, James held her tightly to him. He was so tall, so muscular. She could feel every inch of him against her. She parted her lips invitingly and kissed him again, and again. Then suddenly 'Ouch!' He sprang back, clutching his lower lip where she'd bitten him so hard that she'd drawn blood.

'You can add that to your black eye—won in battle, you might say.' She smoothed herself down, waiting for him to listen to her. 'There's one person you've completely ignored all the way along—and that's Bruce. It's almost as if you don't believe he exists,' she said reprovingly. 'You'd better face it, James, with him around I'm not going to have any interest in you.'

James wiped the blood from his chin. His lip already felt as if it had swollen to three times its normal size. 'Oh yes, Dr Milne—the invisible doctor, you might say. I'm dying to meet him, Nina. I'm curious to discover what this saint of a man's like. It's strange, though,' he went on lightly, 'that no one's ever heard of him. I've talked to a couple of people who go to York regularly for consultations and none of them know him.'

'He's only recently moved to York,' blustered Nina. 'And he obviously travels a lot for his work. You'll meet him soon enough.'

'I look forward to it.' James made a final dab at his lip. 'And when you next see him you can tell him that despite everything, he's still got a rival. Because I'm not giving up on you,' he poked her gently on the shoulder, 'until I find out exactly why you're so unwilling to let anyone get close to you.'

'In that case you'll have a long wait!' Nina called defiantly after him as he opened the door and slipped away. She would never, never tell him. Never.

CHAPTER NINE

NINA stepped back and almost fell off the step-ladder. 'Is that straight?' she asked Angie, who was busy piling books on to shelves.

'I can never tell,' sighed Angie. 'Every day I straighten the picture we've got at the top of our stairs, and it never seems right.'

'It'll just have to do, anyway.' Nina put the hammer in her back pocket and climbed wearily down. 'Well, that's just about it.'

Angie crammed the last book into place, bashed the cardboard box into submission and stood up. 'It's a miracle! I can't believe that this morning everything was just lying around in boxes. Now look at it—you could have been living here for months. Tim and I have been married for two years, yet the boxroom's still full of pictures we've never got round to putting up and rugs we never had the time to put down.'

Nina did a slow twirl, taking in every inch of her new sitting-room. The curtains, which she'd made herself after finding the fabric in a sale, stopped half an inch from the floor, just as she'd calculated. The old pine chest of drawers, which her parents had bought for her as a present, fitted exactly into the alcove by the fireplace and her books and records stacked perfectly on some smart white shelving donated by Anna. The picture she had just hung above the fireplace was the ideal finishing touch, even if it was just a cheap reproduction of a Monet watercolour. She'd been right. From the first moment she'd seen the flat she'd known it was the perfect home for her. It was wise to trust those gut feelings sometimes. 'I can't cook you supper,' she said, rousing her thoughts to concentrate on Angie, who had worked so hard with her all day to help her get the place shipshape. 'The cooker isn't connected and I haven't got any food. But let me treat you to a meal. Let's have a pizza and a bottle of wine as my way of saying thank you.'

'There's nothing I'd like more, honestly, but I've got to go. Tim's got a visiting doctor over from the States and we're all supposed to be going out together.' Angie pulled a face. 'I'd really like to come and celebrate with you—but I *can't*. We'll have to sit around talking medicine all the evening.'

Nina smiled sympathetically, wishing Angie could stay. She needed to spend the evening with someone, perhaps to get a little drunk and celebrate this special day. She didn't, she realised with a rush, want to be left alone in the house with James. Although she'd been planning this move for weeks, and shifted her bits in gradually over days, this morning it had all become permanent. The purchase was complete. She was now the proud owner of this charming residence, and she was sharing a house with James. 'If you have to . . .' She tried to make light of it.

'Come with us,' Angie invited. 'We can talk while the men bore each other to death.'

'I don't think so, thanks all the same.' Somehow all the joy had gone out of the day. She helped Angie pick up a few bits and pieces and take them down to the car. Thanking her again for all her help, Nina walked down the path with her and saw her off. It was funny, but she didn't particularly want to climb the stairs again; didn't want to shut the door on herself and be alone in her new home. She walked from room to room. The kitchen was bright, with red and white curtains she'd chopped down from the old flat. She opened the cupboards one by one. Most of them were empty. Well, she'd soon fill them up with pots and pans and cooking equipment. The shelves would soon groan with home-made jams and pickles and pies. She shuffled the three red and white storage tins on the worktop, seeing which order they looked best in. Why did she suddenly feel so lonely, as if here, above the trees, looking down on the moors in the distance and the roofs close at hand, she was the only person left alive?

There was a strange muffled knocking sound from the direction of her own front door. It sounded ghostly, and she opened it just a slit and peered out. James stood there. He had two glasses in his hand, a bottle of champagne tucked under one arm, and he was holding a package in his other hand. It was obviously the package that he had used to knock with.

'Welcome to your new home.' He waited for her

to open the door wider, but she didn't. 'Nina, please let me in before I drop this lot,' he appealed. She looked him up and down, not sure whether she was pleased to see him or not. He might as well come in, take a look around the place now and begin to realise once and for all that although she was sharing his house, that was the beginning and end of their relationship, she thought. 'Thanks.' He grinned, coming in and taking in the cheap Victorian sketches she'd picked up years ago in a flea market in York. 'You've been working incredibly hard!'

'Angie Sinclair had the day off work, so she's been helping me. Come in.' Nina motioned him towards the sitting-room. 'There's not a lot of furniture, I'm afraid.' There wasn't—just her squashy red chair and the comfy old cane chair with its red and green patterned cushions, plus an old and rather marked coffee table.

'It's better than when *I* started off. I had two old deckchairs and a card table for the first six months. Anyway,' James went on, putting all the things he was carrying on the coffee table and beginning to unpeel the silver paper from around the neck of the champagne bottle, 'let's drink to your happiness here. I know you don't need any help, and I know that if you did, Dr Milne would be here to give you a hand . . .' There was a satisfying pop as he deftly rotated the bottle around the cork, which came away gently. 'Is Dr Milne here, by the way?' He looked round the room as if he expected Bruce Milne to jump out of a cupboard.

'No,' muttered Nina, wondering how she was going to get herself out of this mess. Nothing good ever came of telling lies, even if they seemed quite innocent ones at the time. 'He's . . . er . . . he won't be here for a few days yet. He's got to make his own arrangements.'

'Will he be here next Saturday?' James asked solicitously, pouring her a glass of bubbly and handing it gently to her. She felt annoyance with him creeping over her. He'd just walked in, taken over—he hadn't even bothered to ask her if she wanted a glass of champagne.

'Oh yes,' she said with feigned confidence.

'In that case you're both invited to a party, here—downstairs.' James raised his glass to her. 'Welcome to Arcadia Gardens. I hope we'll be good neighbours.'

'Oh, *I* will. I like to keep myself to myself,' she responded hastily. He sat lazily in the cane chair, one of his legs dangling over the arm, and although the fact that he obviously felt so much at home infuriated her she couldn't help but also welcome the company. In a way he was her first guest here, even if he was uninvited.

'I was thinking about next Saturday,' he said, looking thoughtfully at her. 'Why don't you invite your friends and make it a kind of flat-warming, and I'll have my friends. We can use the whole house, and if the weather's nice we can use the garden too. I could get some of those special garden flares to light the place up . . . It could be very nice,' he mused. 'Don't you think so? And you could invite more people than you could fit comfortably into this flat.' She looked at him expressionlessly. 'I'd be grateful, to be honest, Nina. I don't know that many people from the hospital. I'll be having some friends up from London and some old school friends too, but I'd really appreciate the chance to meet some others.'

'OK.' If she said no, Nina thought to herself, it would sound suspicious; if she invited a huge crowd of friends and Dr Milne just failed to turn up James probably wouldn't notice. And if he saw her in a crowd of her own friends he might get the message that she didn't need him.

'Good.' He smiled. 'And now a little house-warming present.' He handed her the package. It was wrapped, none too neatly, she noted, in stylish paper—and it weighed several pounds.

'I can't,' she protested. 'It's nice of you, but——' She stopped short, aware that his smile had grown even wider.

'Go on,' He was watching her intently. 'You just said something positive about me. Keep going, while you can think of something good to say.' Nina tried to force herself to be angry with him, but for some reason she couldn't. He was being so nice, so considerate. Of course, he was only doing it for his own purposes. He was just trying to show her up. She tried to rouse herself against him, but nothing happened. The thought that it was a long time since a man had been kind to her loomed large in her mind.

'It's very kind of you, James,' she managed. 'But I can't possibly . . .'

'Why not?' he enquired, watching her like a hawk. 'Haven't some of your other friends given you housewarming presents? Did you turn them down?'

'Yes—no . . . It's different. *We're* not friends.'

'This is my peace offering, so that we *can* be friends in the future. Take it. I hope you like it,' he said quietly. 'Please, Nina. Open it. You've kicked me and bitten me, but it would hurt me more than even that if you refused to accept this.'

Nina weighed the package in her hands, curious, desperately wanting to know what was in it yet scared of what it would mean if she opened it. To accept it would be like an admission that she was accepting him. She wanted to find some way of saying sorry for losing her temper with him last time, and the time before—but once she started being weak, once she began to apologise she knew, with absolute certainty, that she'd be lost. Anna's words weighed heavily on her ears. *The lady doth protest too much*, Anna had chided when Nina had got home and told her about their row in the broom cupboard. Nina looked across at him. He was so attractive. But Alan Gill had been attractive too, and kind, and loving. 'No,' she said firmly.

James took the gift from her lap. His eyes seemed suddenly clouded. 'All right, I'll open it for you.' He tore off the paper that he'd only stuck in place a few minutes ago. It came away to reveal an object wrapped in protective plastic bubble-paper.

That he pulled away too. A marble cherub, about twelve inches high, was revealed. Its legs were missing; it had a beautiful child's face, with rounded arms and plump little shoulders. Two feathery wings sprouted from its back. James balanced it on his hand. The arms reached out and there was a mischievous twist to its smile, as if it had just done something naughty. 'It's Italian, about five hundred years old.' He ran his fingers affectionately over the curls in the carved hair. 'I'm sorry it's damaged, but if it hadn't been I wouldn't have been able to buy it.' Nina gazed at it, wanting to touch it and not daring to do so. It was beautiful. It was the most beautiful thing she'd ever seen. James put it down on the coffee table.

'I thought you could do with a guardian angel to keep an eye on you and make sure you don't get into any more scrapes. It's not a very serious angel, as you can see. It would let you do a bit of picketing at the local cinema, and other things like that, but it would draw the line at letting you get into serious trouble.' He patted it sadly on the head. 'I'll be off. It's yours, Nina, it was meant for you. I'll see you around.' He was almost out of the door when she spoke.

'James.' He stopped but didn't turn round. One sharp word from her now, he vowed, and he would give up. He couldn't go on giving to her without receiving anything in return. 'Thank you.' Her voice was quiet. 'I don't know what to say. It's the most perfect gift I've ever been given.' She thought for a minute he was going to walk out, and her conscience tore at her. A man who didn't care about her would have bought flowers or jewellery or perfume, or something that women were traditionally supposed to like. But this was something from the heart, something intensely personal. And she'd never given him anything except a hard time. Not even a willing kiss. 'I'm sorry.' Her voice shook. 'You know it's not easy for me—you're so kind, and I've done nothing to deserve it.'

'That's all right. You're easy to forgive.' James turned, his hands thrust into his jeans pockets. 'Look, Nina, I don't know a lot about you, but I want you to remember something. I know what it's like to get hurt and feel that you'll never trust anyone again. But you *can* trust me. I'll be there if you need me, I promise.' And then he did walk out on her, and despite the cherub's naughty smile and the fact that it was the first night in her own home, Nine broke down and wept.

The party was going well—better than she'd hoped, Nina thought, edging her way through the hall and into James's sitting-room after giving yet another necessarily brief guided tour of her flat. There must have been a hundred people there, in the garden and on the stairs, crammed into the front room where loud music was playing and everyone was dancing. 'All right?' James fought his way towards her, a bottle of wine in each hand, filling the glasses of those who were standing still long enough to have a drink. Nina nodded. It was a good party, and a lot of that was his doing. People liked James. She realised with a sense of foreboding that *she* probably had more than her fair share of detractors. 'No sign of Bruce Milne?' He seemed to be watching her response very closely.

'No!' she yelled above the noise. 'I expect he was called out on an emergency.'

He looked at her very strangely. 'Do endocrinologists have emergencies? I thought they spent their time in consulting rooms or hunched over laboratory benches.' Nina could have hit herself. What a stupid mistake to make! Endocrinologists specialised in hormones; they spent their time helping stunted children to grow tall and imbalanced women to have children. They worked miracles, but they weren't called out in the middle of the night to attend a bedside. She pretended not to hear him, but James saw the flicker of desperation that crossed her face. Before he could say anything the doorbell rang, and he plunged out into the hall to answer it.

Nina went through to the kitchen. A little knot of men were discussing cricket and another knot, this time of women, most of them nurses, were discussing the pros and cons of new mothers eating their placenta to help replace the hormones lost in the afterbirth. Neither conversation appealed to her, so she stood alone, resting against one of the oak kitchen units until something more interesting happened—which it soon did. 'Nina!' James came bounding towards her. 'He's here!'

'Who?' asked Nina, thrown for a moment.

'Bruce Milne.' A tall man, taller than James,

walked into the kitchen. He was dark and so excessively good-looking that the nurses immediately stopped talking and fixed their eyes longingly on him. He was dressed like a film star too, in an off-white linen suit that was glamorously crumpled. What was more, he was heading towards her with a confident smile, as if he knew her well.

'Nina darling . . .' He bent and kissed her familiarly on the cheek, then put his arm possessively round her shoulders. 'I'm sorry I'm so late. You know what it's like.' She wondered for a moment whether she had gone completely mad. It was the only explanation. Bruce Milne didn't exist. He was a figment of her imagination. She had made him up, completely off the top of her head, out of Bruce Springsteen and A. A. Milne. He *couldn't* exist. But his arm squeezing her shoulder said entirely the opposite. Glancing across at James, she saw him regarding them under lowered brows, as if he didn't approve. If *he* believed that this was Bruce Milne, what did it matter? At least she had a man here, real, living and breathing and breathtakingly handsome—exactly what she had planned when she'd created him to keep James at bay.

'Of course I do,' she responded with what she hoped was a loving look. Slinging her arm in as casual a fashion as possible around his waist, she smiled knowingly at James. 'Have you been properly introduced to James Farris, who owns the house?'

'Yes, he let me in.' Bruce shook hands with James, who looked as if he wasn't feeling too well.

'Thanks for looking after her so well while I wasn't around. Nina's told me how kind you've been. I hope that now I'm here she'll keep out of trouble.' He bent and kissed her again, this time on the lips. Nina didn't really like it—it was like kissing a total stranger. 'Would you get me a drink, darling?'

Well, she thought, trying to find a clean glass while the enigmatic Dr Milne stood chatting to James, this wasn't quite what she'd intended him to be like. The imaginary Dr Milne would have got his own drink, not sent her off like a lackey. She pondered what could be happening as she poured out a glass of Alsace wine. There were two alternatives. Either she was having a nervous breakdown or she'd subliminally known about Bruce Milne all the time. Maybe he *was* an endocrinologist at York. Maybe she'd met him while she'd been there, and perhaps in the chaos that had followed Alan's confession she'd blanked him out of her mind. Then she'd seen that record and book, those names, and thrown the two of them together. It didn't make sense, but then some of the strangest things were true. Trying to look as if she knew the man intimately, she walked smilingly back to his side and settled against him when he replaced his arm around her.

'Thanks, baby,' he murmured dismissively, then turned his attention back to the other people he was talking to—about cricket. Nina tried not to let her annoyance show on her face. She smiled inanely at James, who smiled wanly back. He'd lost her, that was what his expression said. Nina felt a pang of regret, particularly when Bruce Milne's hand curved surreptitiously round her breast. She held her breath. This couldn't be happening! She stared up at his lean face with its fashionable sprinkling of stubble. This wasn't what she'd wanted—not some groper who couldn't keep his hands to himself even in public. The feeling of panic that she'd experienced when she'd first seen him surged again in her as she realised that the whole situation was beyond her control. This man could do what he wanted with her, because in front of James she couldn't argue, couldn't protest. She was supposed to be in love with him, blissfully happy in his company.

'Come on, let's dance,' he told her, rousing her from her thoughts. And he led her as if she was some kind of dog out of the kitchen and into the sitting-room, where he placed one hand around her waist and the other across her shoulders and held her plastered against him for the entire duration of a smoochy Lionel Ritchie number. 'Mmm,' he murmured in her ear as he kissed her neck. Nina tried not to shrink from him, determined that no one should guess the nightmare that was going on. His hands crept round to her breast once more, and in the dark he began to caress her. She stiffened, held herself as far away from him as she could and wondered what was going on. When was it going to end? Perhaps she was asleep, dreaming, and she'd wake up—but no, his hands on her, mauling her like a piece of meat, weren't a dream. The record ended, but he still held her. The next one was a fast

bop, and everyone in the room released their part-
ners—everyone except him. 'Come on,' he whispered, pulling her tight against his pelvis. 'It's a
long time since I saw you, Nina. Let's go upstairs
and say hallo properly. I'm sure we can find somewhere quiet for half an hour.' He seemed to feel her
stiffen in his arms. 'Relax!' he laughed, but she
wasn't amused. Blind panic swept over her. Whoever this man was, whether she'd met him before or
whether he was a figment of her imagination, she
didn't like him. She had to get away from him
before he did something awful—but already he was
hauling her up the stairs, past curious and amused
people from the hospital, who were more used to
seeing her in conversation or argument than being
swept away to a bedroom by a handsome man.

'Don't start playing hard to get, darling,' he
muttered, opening a door on the landing and pulling her in. While he fumbled for the light switch
Nina managed to wrench herself free and put a
couple of yards between them. Then she stumbled
over something on the floor, and as the light went
on overhead found herself sprawled across a
double bed. 'That's better.' Bruce Milne bent over
her, smoothing back the hair from her face.

He ran his fingers down her throat, where the
burn caused by Tony Brewer had all but disappeared, then began to slide apart the buttons at
the front of her dress. Nina lay there for a second
like a rabbit paralysed with terror, watching his
beautiful hands open one button after the other.
And then the old energy and fury came back to her,

and she slapped him as hard as she could across the face. He recoiled and staggered across the room, and she saw the mask of confidence slide from his face for a second.

'Who *are* you?' she demanded, sitting up and gathering her dress around her.

'Bruce Milne,' he said, but without much conviction.

'Bruce Milne doesn't exist. I made him up.' She glared at him. 'Tell me, who are you?'

'My name's Charlie Oldham.' His voice had changed. Now he had a slight Scottish accent instead of that milk chocolate drawl. He held out his hands imploringly towards her, then thought better of it and put them in his pockets. 'Nina, I'm so sorry. I was hoping you'd stop me sooner, but no matter what I did you didn't seem to object. James said that——'

'James?' Nina couldn't believe it.

'James is an old friend of mine, from university days. When he knew I was coming he asked me to pretend to be someone called Bruce Milne—I don't know why, it sounded like a joke at the time. All I was supposed to do was come in and act boorishly towards you so that we could have a big argument.' He sighed. 'He said that if we had a big row it would help him, and the surest way to provoke a fight was to . . . Well, to be physical.' He shook his head apologetically. 'I'm sorry. I kept hoping all that time down in the kitchen you'd start to yell and shout at me, but nothing happened. I was behaving as badly as I could, and you just took it all stoically.' He scratched his head. 'Look, it's not too late. We can have a row now if you want. You can throw me out of here if it'll help.'

Nina's hands shook. Her voice seemed to come from a long way away. 'No, it's not your fault. I'm going to go and find James and kill him.' The door opened silently.

'I've come to give myself up.' James edged round the room, as if Nina was going to explode and his best chance of survival was to stick to the walls. 'Thanks, Charlie.' He tried to smile. 'I've got a lot of explaining to do to Nina.'

'I'll see you later. Look, I'm awfully sorry.' Looking totally bewildered, Charlie Oldham, or Bruce Milne, or whoever he was, made a swift exit.

There was a long silence as the two adversaries eyed each other up like gladiators planning a fight to the death. 'Before I tear you apart limb from limb,' Nina said at last, 'I'd like you to explain why you played such a dirty, despicable trick on me.' She buttoned up her dress as she spoke; it was a loose-cut one with a dropped waist, and she'd suddenly realised that without her bra James, and Charlie too, had probably enjoyed a glimpse of her bosom. 'Why, James? I'd really begun to believe all that rubbish you'd spun about us being friends.' The hurt in her eyes made him want to just fold her in his arms—a mistake, he knew. She'd be like a tigress.

'Because I love you. Why can't you understand that?' He stared at her helplessly. 'A couple of

weeks ago I began to doubt the existence of Bruce
Milne. I'd never seen him, there was no evidence
that he existed. Nothing rang true about him, nothing! Why would an eminent endocrinologist from
York want to share a pokey flat with you here? And
why wouldn't he give you a share in the cost of the
mortgage? He never came here to help you, and
when I mentioned him to Anna she was surprised
and said she'd never heard of him either. So it
dawned on me that you'd invented him as an excuse
to keep me at a distance.'

'And so you decided to get your friend to assault
me tonight?' Nina took a handful of the loose-
woven bedcover and squeezed it in her hands.
'You're warped!'

'No more warped than you, letting Charlie kiss
you and . . .' James dried up and stared moodily at
the carpet. 'I couldn't believe my eyes. I thought
the minute he told you to go and get him a drink
you'd tell him where to go, but you just did it. You
wouldn't have done it for me.' He squatted down
and traced a pattern in the wool pile with the tip of
his index finger while he cleared his throat. 'And
then there you were dancing, and he was like an
octopus . . .'

'All right,' Nina interrupted. 'Why did you do
it?'

'Because I knew that you'd never admit Bruce
Milne didn't exist. What's more, I knew that if I
even mentioned the fact that I didn't believe in him
you'd use it as an excuse for a row. I didn't want to
jeopardise the progress I'd made with you so far. I

figured that if Charlie came along, introduced himself as Bruce Milne and then engineered a row with you it would get us both out of the impasse. I could step in and rescue you, you would have proved to everyone that he *did* exist, but he'd be out of the way. No one would have lost their pride.' James laughed bitterly. 'It sounds ridiculous now, but it made sense at the time. I didn't think you'd go along with it. I thought the moment he laid a hand on you you'd lash out.'

There was a long, long silence. James stayed crouched on the floor at the end of the bed while Nina kneaded the bedspread like a cat. She just felt stunned, shocked by what he had told her. And she realised what a fool she had made herself look by inventing Bruce Milne in the first place. What was even more shocking was the fact that now James was here and within her reach, most of her anger seemed to have melted away. All she could think of was Charlie Oldham pawing her, and James watching, waiting for the explosion—and nothing had happened. No wonder he'd looked so wan!

'I've got to know, Nina. Why were you prepared to let him touch you and not me?' James's voice was hoarse. 'If you can tell me honestly that you hate me or find me repulsive I'll accept it and go away quietly.' There was another pause, broken only by whoops and the pounding beat from downstairs. 'But I think there's something else. Anna said something the other night, something I didn't understand, about you taking a long time to recover from things.'

'I thought Anna was my friend!' yelped Nina.

'She is, you idiot, and so am I!' James slapped the floor. 'Don't you understand that if we weren't your friends we'd have given up on you long ago?'

'Some friend you've turned out to be!'

He got to this feet and looked over her. 'Just one answer, Nina, that's all. Why could Charlie do this—' he kissed her and she flinched away, 'and this?' He put his arm around her shoulder and held her to him, feeling her tremble against his skin. He went no further. 'When a total stranger does that you just stand there smiling at him. But when I do it it's as if I'm hurting you. Why? It's all I want to know.'

Nina gulped hard, trying to hold back the tears that always threatened to engulf her when he held her. How could she tell him? It was too humiliating . . . He kissed her again, slowly, and she tried to push him away, but he held hard. She twisted her face, but he pulled her back. 'You can tell me.'

'No, I can't,' she cried.

'Is it *that* awful?' He seemed to laugh at her. 'If it's something so bad then you need to speak to someone about it.'

'All right.' She looked at him defiantly. 'In fact, it's nothing very remarkable at all. You'll be embarrassed when you hear what you've been making such a fuss about. I met a man, a couple of years ago. He was friendly and kind, and I fell in love with him. I thought he loved me too. We were going to set up home together . . .'

She began to cry, great rasping sobs that racked

her body. James gathered her up in his arms and finished the story. 'And just when you thought it was going to be happy ever after you found that everything you'd believed in, everything you'd planned, was false.' He hugged her to him, and this time she didn't resist. 'And for all this time you've been determined that no one's ever going to hurt you like that again. And the only way to make sure that it doesn't happen is to keep away from anyone who might tempt you to get involved. I'm right, aren't I?' He took Nina's hiccup for agreement. 'So the people you could fall in love with you keep at arm's length. It's all right.' He rocked her until her sobs began to subside. 'I know all about it. All I can say is that you're damned lucky I'm a stubborn kind of man. Feeling better?'

Nina peered up at him blurrily. He was smiling tenderly at her. 'Yes,' she admitted. His arms around her were comforting, not threatening any more. 'I don't deserve you.' Her words were almost smothered against his chest. 'All the time I was being so nasty to you I knew it was because . . .' She was silent.

'Yes?' He tormented her with a questioning look.

'Because part of me liked you. All right,' she protested when he looked disgustedly at her, 'because for the past three weeks I knew I was falling in love with you, and nothing I did seemed to stop it. Have you heard what you wanted to hear?'

James nodded and then bent to kiss her. 'Now we've both come clean, what do we do? If I were to promise not to pay any more visits to the Regal Cinema do you think you could bear to live with me? It's odd—I feel I know you so well, better than someone I've known for years. When I saw you for the first time I knew it had to be you.'

Nina grinned. 'And then you met me!'

James nodded philosophically. 'And despite the tongue-lashing you gave me, and the split lip since, I remained convinced, most of the time, that I wanted you.' He kissed her deeply, pressing her back against the pillows, and she didn't flinch or move away. 'I still want you. Badly.' His hand was pressed against her ribcage, his thumb encroaching on ground that not so long ago Charlie Oldham had covered.

Nina held his hand to her breast. 'You can have me. James,' she paused, stopping his kisses, 'just tell me that you're not married and that you don't intend to marry anyone—except me, of course. I'd feel better if you would.'

'I'm not, I don't, and if that was a proposal I accept.' He watched fascinated as she waited a few seconds, as if something was going to happen. 'What's wrong?'

'Nothing. I was just waiting for my guardian angel to strike you down with a thunderbolt if you were telling lies,' she laughed. 'Look, this is ridiculous, we're supposed to be hosting a party downstairs. We can't spend the evening cooped up in here.' She went to get up from the bed. 'There's time for this later, if you're serious about it.' James groaned.

'You're right, there's plenty of time later. Now we've got to go down and try to explain everything to Charlie.'

Nina stroked his hair. 'Tell me once more that you're going to stay.'

'It's no good, Sister Newington,' James said gravely. 'I've given up some of the best weeks of my life winning the Moorside shrew, and now I've got her I'm never going to let her go. No matter how much she may regret it.' Nina batted him around the ear. 'Or *I* regret getting involved with a liberated woman . . .'

Bestselling Author Carole Mortimer's latest title 'WITCHCHILD'.

A heart-rending tale of break-up and reconciliation.
Millionaire 'Hawk' Sinclair mistakenly accuses novelist
Leonie Spencer of ruthlessly pursuing his son Hal for a share
in the family fortune.

It's actually a case of mistaken identity, but as a
consequence the bewitching Leonie finds herself caught up
in a maelstrom of passion, blackmail and kidnap.

Available November 1987 Price: £2.95

W❂RLDWIDE

From Boots, Martins, John Menzies, W H Smith,
Woolworths and other paperback stockists.